SYDNEY
SCANDAL

By Judy Katschke

Illustrations by
Tom Bancroft and Rob Corley

Published by KidsGive, LLC.
5757 W. Century Blvd., Suite 800, Box 8
Los Angeles, California 90045

Karito Kids®, Karito® and KidsGive® are trademarks of KidsGive, LLC.

Cover art by Funny Pages Productions, LLC
(Tom Bancroft, Rob Corley, and Jon Conkling)
Interior illustrations by Funny Pages Productions, LLC
(Tom Bancroft and Rob Corley)
Text layout by Jason T. Hill
Journal written & designed by Jason T. Hill

ISBN-13: 978-09792912-6-5

KidsGive
5757 W. Century Blvd. Suite 800, Box 8
Los Angeles, California 90045

Printed in China. First printing, 2008.

Visit Karito Kids at karitokids.com.

your code number
is

895572001056

....

You can go online to help kids around the world right now... here's how!

Go to **karitokids.com** and select **ACTIVATION**. Enter the activation number above, then choose a cause to help another child, whether it is food, home, school or health.

Once you've entered your special code in the activation section, you officially become a **Karito Kids® World Citizen™**. Congratulations on joining an exciting new community of kids who care!

You can choose to get updates on your project sent to you and find out how you have truly made a difference.

What Is Karito Kids® all about?

We launched Karito Kids® to help connect children around the world in a number of ways.

- The word "Karito" means charity and love of one's neighbor in the constructed language Esperanto. We hope that children around the world strengthen their connection with each other, creating a global village of peace and understanding.

- Each Karito Kids doll helps children recognize and appreciate the beauty of the world's many different ethnicities.

- The book that accompanies each Karito Kid tells a fun story involving that girl. It brings to life another country and its culture and connects readers to the notion that children from across the world have many fundamental similarities.

- The unique online activation process will allow children to directly participate in giving. They can determine the cause to which they wish to direct a percentage of the purchase price of the product. They can receive updates on the project they choose and find out how they helped children somewhere else in the world.

- Combining traditional play with innovative interactive games provides your child a play date with kids all over the world. They will have the opportunity to learn how children live in other parts of the world.

- Our selected charity, Plan, is a non-profit organization that is bringing hope and help to more than 10 million children and their families in poor communities worldwide. KidsGive contributes 3% of the retail price to one charity to maximize the impact of change.

fun stuff to do with this book:

Help other kids and find out more about the characters and their countries!

To help another kid, all you have to do is go to **www.karitokids.com** and activate your donation by putting in your special code found on page 3. Three percent of the price of this book will be donated by us to a children's charity called Plan. The best part is that you get to choose how you want to help!

While you're reading this book, keep track of places in the book where another country or culture is mentioned. Make sure that you enter them at **www.karitokids. com**, and you'll earn stamps and points in your on-line passport.

You can find out more about each character by playing

games set in scenes from the character's world. Go to **www.karitokids.com** and click on Hidden Quest.

Play other games and find out about all the Karito Kids® by going to **www.karitokids.com**!

CHAPTER 1

"G'day!" I said. "Pipper the Nipper to the rescue!"

The sunbaking bloke floating on the raft opened one eye. Then both eyes grew wide. I guess he was surprised to see an eleven-year-old kid wearing a striped cap and paddling over on a surfboard!

"But...I was not drowning!" he said.

No surprise that the guy had an accent. There are always heaps of tourists from all over the world on Bondi Beach!

"But you did fall asleep on your raft, mate," I explained. "I know it's still early but another hour of sunbaking and you'll be as red as a Tasmanian crab!"

"Danke!" the guy said as I paddled away. I think that's German for thanks. But hey, it's all in a days work for me—Pipper the Ripper Nipper!

You see, Pip is a nickname for my real name, Piper. Ripper means "great" here in my

7

country, Australia, and Nippers are junior surf lifesavers. We meet early every Sunday morning to learn beach safety and lifesaving techniques. Okay, warning a guy to use sunscreen isn't exactly pulling a person trapped in a killer rip, but someday I'll do that, and hopefully real, real soon!

As I paddled back to shore I felt the spring sun beating down on my cap. The stripes make Nippers easy to spot in the ocean. We also wear rashies, which are light skintight suits that cover our bodies and arms. When we really feel

like stylin' we wear boardies, neat board shorts in all colors. My favorite pair is orange and blue. Oh, and sunscreen. Always heaps of sunscreen!

Being a Nipper is fun, but the best part about learning how to be a surf lifesaver is surfing. And I surf any chance I get.

Like right now!

"Ye-es!" I cheered as I glanced back. The perfect glassy wave was swelling right behind me.

I positioned myself to hang five. That's surfing with five toes hanging off the front of the board. Someday I'll hang ten but only when my feet are much bigger!

I could feel my heart pounding as the wave swelled under my board. That's the best part, because it's what always happens right before you *take off!*

"Woo-hoooo!" I cheered.

As the wave carried me forward I was totally stoked—even after I wiped out and landed in the soup with a huge *splash!*

But hey, surfing is just like life. It's got its ups and it's got its downs. So I climbed back on my board. Instead of surfing, though, I paddled straight to Bondi Beach.

It was still early but the beach was already

filling with tourists, locals and Surfies like me. One of the things that makes Bondi so cool is that it's only seven kilometers—about four miles—from the center of Australia's oldest and biggest city—Sydney!

I live with my mum, Jill, my dad, Ron, and my eight-year-old sister, Elly. Lucky for me our house is in a suburb right near the beach. It has a bright red roof and a barbie (barbecue) in the front yard. Australians love to barbecue any chance we get. Oh, and we don't eat kangaroo meat! Just lots of grilled veggies and shrimp!

As I lifted my board out of the water, I heard someone call, "Oi, Pipper!"

I looked up and saw the Age Manager, Zac, the leader of my Nipper Group. When Zac wasn't teaching us safety, first aid and coaching beach games, he was a real-live surf lifesaver on Bondi!

"You know you're not supposed to leave the group, Pip," Zac said. "Especially to go in the water!"

I shaded my eyes from the sun as I looked up at Zac. His black sunnies covered his eyes, and he wore zinc oxide on his nose. But he was not wearing a smile.

"Sorry, Zac, but the guy was in danger," I said.

"He needed my help straight away!"

My little sister Elly came running over.

"I saw you out there, Pip!" Elly said, jumping up and down in the sand excitedly. "Was that man drowning? Was he caught in a rip? Was he too tired to swim?"

I stared at Elly. It wasn't easy having a little sister who thought you were some kind of hero. Especially when you knew you weren't!

"Let's just say he had burning issues," I sighed.

Elly wrinkled her nose as if she didn't get it. Then with a shrug she ran back to her Nipper group's potato sack race.

"When do I get to save someone from drowning, Zac?" I asked. "I've been a Nipper since I was five years old!"

"After you learn surf safety, surf awareness and surf skills," Zac explained gently. "In the meantime, your job is to have fun."

"I am having fun," I said. I really was—until I remembered something I had forgotten to do!

"Rats!" I said, whacking my forehead with my palm. "I forgot to tell that bloke to recycle his sunscreen bottles!"

Zac smiled as he tilted his head. "I knew you

were a Surfie, Pip," he said. "But I didn't know you were a Greenie too."

"And proud of it!" I said with a smile. "Hey, if I can't save a person from drowning, I can still save the earth!"

I wanted to tell Zac all about the cool club I belonged to after school called Mean and Green. And how my friends and I spread the word on everything from recycling to saving wildlife. But Zac was already rounding up our group for a run on the beach.

I lay my surfboard on the sand next to the other Nippers' boards. Then I fell in line with my Nipper mates. Like me, they were stoked it was spring holiday. Spring for Australian kids comes in late September. Because we're the Land Down Under (under the equator) our seasons are flip-flopped with Europe and the States. So while American kids are building snowmen, Aussie kids are building sandcastles!

But as we started to sprint I didn't see many castles in the sand at all—just crumpled lolly (candy) wrappers, icypole (popsicle) sticks and empty plastic water bottles.

"Gross!" I complained, stopping to pick up a water bottle. Didn't people know it took about four hundred years for a plastic water bottle to break down?

Zac must have seen me because he shouted, "Keep up with the group, Pip!"

"I'm coming, Zac!" I called back. *Right after I throw out this bottle!*

My group raced ahead as I went looking for a recycle bin. The air was heavy with coconut sunscreen as I zigzagged my way around sunbakers, beach-volleyball players and picnickers on the sand.

How could anyone toss away his rubbish when there weren't any recycling bins? I scribbled a mental note inside my head to bring it up with my Mean and Green club when I got back to school.

Then finally I saw it—a recycling bin on a secluded part of the beach. I hurried over to it and lifted the lid. But as I tossed the bottle inside, I eyed something big and bulky lying near the water. *An empty plastic rubbish bag!* I groaned. "Do I have to pick up everybody's rubbish?" I said, shaking my head.

I walked toward the bag and noticed something weird. It was moving up and down as if it was breathing!

Too weird.

Slowly I made my way across the wet sand to the heaving object. That's when I saw that the bulky thingy on the beach was no bag at all.

"Jingoes!" I gasped. "It's a beached whale!"

CHAPTER 2

I didn't have to run to find Zac because he was running back to find me.

"Pip!" Zac said. "Didn't we just talk about—"

"Look!" I cut in.

Zac turned in the direction I was pointing. Then he knew exactly what to do. He rung up a volunteer wildlife rescue group. In less than a half an hour, they were on the scene!

"Why is he so small?" I asked one of the rescuers as they gently poured buckets of water on the whale. "I thought whales were huge."

"This one looks like a baby beluga," she answered. "The poor thing is disoriented."

"Dis-what?" I asked.

"Confused," she explained.

At least he was still alive. I stepped back to let the rescuers do their job. By now, more and more people were crowding on the beach near the whale. It was still heaving as it lay sprawled on the wet sand.

"I wonder what happened to its mother," a woman behind me said.

"I hope they can help it," a man said.

But the two girls next to me didn't seem so worried. They were identical twins, and they looked very posh (rich). One wore a leopard-print two-piece cozzy (swimsuit) with a gold charm ankle bracelet. The other's cozzie was plain black but with strands of pink and white shell-necklaces. They both wore gigantic sunnies that made them look like hoot-owls and sunhats with their names stitched on the brims: Lucy and Darcy.

"Is he sick?" Darcy asked.

I shook my head and said, "They say he's confused."

"Well, he looks sick to me," Lucy said. She turned to her sister. "Great, Darcy. The last thing we need on spring holiday is some fish disease!"

"Whales are mammals, not fish," I said.

"It smells like a fish!" Lucy said, wrinkling her nose.

I pressed my lips together to keep from screaming. Didn't they know that it was humans who made sea creatures sick—by spilling chemicals and junk into the water?

Those twins may be posh, I decided. *But they're not Greenies.*

I moved away from the twins as I watched the

rescuers lift the whale onto the flatbed of a large truck. The crowd on the beach cheered as the whale was driven away, happy that he was going to get the help he needed. I was happy too but also worried. How was the baby whale beached in the first place? And would it happen to another whale?

By the time the crowd broke up, the sun was high in the sky. Zac told us Nippers to call it a day. "Ripper job, Nippers," he told us. "We'll finish that run next week. Hopefully there'll be no beached whales on the way."

Hopefully is right! As I picked up my surfboard, most of the kids were running to their mums or dads waiting nearby. It's a Nipper rule that one parent has to be on the beach while we train.

No problem for me—my Dad runs the Whelan's Surf Shack and is on the beach almost every day! When the surf shop opened over fifty years ago, business was good. But now that more surf shacks are popping up, Dad has to work extra hard.

"Hi, Dad!" I called as I walked over the sand to the surf shack. A row of longboards and shortboards stood in their racks. Most of them had the coolest designs like flames, flowers—even favorite Australian animals like koalas!

"Hey, Pipper!" Dad said, smiling. "Save anyone

today?" He leaned over the counter where he also sold sunscreen and sunnies. There was even a spinning rack of Bondi Beach travel pamphlets— compliments of my mum, who had quit working at the surf shop to become a travel agent.

"I saved a sunbaked German tourist," I said as I leaned my surfboard against the rack. "And a beached baby whale."

Dad pushed his sunnies up on his head. Being out in the sun every day was making his fair hair even fairer!

"I heard about that whale," Dad said. "But I

couldn't leave the shack to check it out."

"It was a bummer, Dad!" I said. "I wish I knew more about whales so I could try to help them."

"That's my Pip," Dad said with a smile. "Remember when you tried saving the lobsters from the seafood restaurant?"

"I had to!" I said. "They were still alive!"

Dad nodded as if he got it. But Mum doesn't see the world through green-colored glasses. In fact, she's always telling me, "You can't save the whole world, Pip."

True. But maybe I can save a little bit of Australia!

And why not? We Whelans have been living in the Land Down Under for over 300 years. Okay, it's not as long as the Aboriginal People who have lived in Australia for 40,000 years, but a few hundred years is a pretty good run!

Anyway, back in the 1700's my great-great-great-can't-keep track-grandfather Benjamin Whelan was brought over from Ireland on a convict ship for stealing a cow. I like to think he was just borrowing the cow to feed his hungry family. Heaps of Aussies have ancestors who came over that way.

The convicts could have gone back after they

finished their time, but I guess when they saw the awesome beaches, the fascinating people, and the amazing animals and felt the great weather, they decided to stick around. Hey, can't blame them!

As for Mum, she's a true first generation Aussie. Her own mum came here from Italy and her dad from what is now the Czech Republic. Like Australia, I'm a hodgepodge of different cultures!

"I'd better wax some boards," Dad said. He grabbed a jar of surfboard wax and stepped out of the shack.

I leaned against the counter, spinning the travel brochure rack. There were brochures for Kakadu National Park with its crocodiles, wallabies and dingos, and Ayers Rock, a huge red rock in the middle of Australia. Almost all of the brochures had pictures of kangaroos on them. Tourists love seeing real-live 'roos in Australia. Then I found one brochure that made my eyes totally bug out. "The Great Barrier Reef!" I gasped.

I grabbed the brochure and flipped through it. The last time my family went to the Great Barrier Reef, I was seven. I never forgot snorkeling under the water and seeing hundreds of awesome fish and coral. And now that I had earned my scuba diving certificate in the local swimming pool, it was definitely time to go back!

"Dad!" I said, waving the brochure. "Can we go to the Great Barrier Reef?"

"Sorry, Pip," Dad said. "But your mum and I can't take off from work right now."

"Is business that bad?" I asked.

Dad stopped waxing to stare out at the beach. "It's a little slow today," he sighed. "Maybe all the tourists went whale watching instead."

Whale watching?

That's it! If I couldn't go to the Great Barrier Reef, I'd go whale watching. I could find out more about whales—and maybe help them, too.

"Can I go whale watching today, Dad?" I asked.

Dad was about to answer when a family of four walked over to the shack.

"Pardonez-moi," the woman said in French. "We

21

would like some…how you say…surfing boards."

"Well, you've come to the right place, mates!" Dad declared. "We've got surfboards in all weights and sizes—even boogie boards for the wee ones."

Dad seemed happy to have the business. And I was happy for Dad. But he still didn't answer my question!

"Dad?" I asked again. "Can I go whale-watching?"

"Sure, Pip, sure," Dad said over his shoulder.

"Cool!" I said. It was all systems go!

I spun the pamphlet rack and pulled out a few brochures for whale watching cruises. As I flipped through them I walked down the beach toward the closest marina.

There were all sorts of whale-watching cruises. One was called "Whale of a Tour." It looked like a big party boat serving food and punch. Another cruise, which handed out whale-shaped hats and taught passengers how to sing sea shanties, was called "Blubber Brigade." There was even a super fancy cruise that had the nerve to serve caviar, which were fish eggs! But they all had one thing in common—they were expensive!

Reaching into my pouch I pulled out a five-dollar note. It was enough for a few icypoles but not enough for a whale-watching cruise.

"Who am I joshin'?" I sighed. "I don't even have

enough to buy one of those corny whale hats."

I was about to put away my money when something red and green swooped down in front of my face.

"Arrrrrk!"

It was a parrot!

I gasped as it flapped its wings, lifted its claws and snatched the five-dollar note right out of my hands!

"Hey!" I shouted.

"Raaaak!" the parrot squawked as he shot off.

"Stop thief!" I cried.

I spun to chase the bird. *Crash!* My teeth rattled inside my head as I bumped into something—or someone. Looking up, I saw a dark-haired man grinning down at me. Over one eye was a black eye patch. On top of his head was a tri-cornered plumed hat. Perched on one broad shoulder was that fine-feathered bandit with my five-dollar note!

"Arrgh!" the man growled. "Lookin' for someone, lassie?"

I gulped hard. It was a pirate!

CHAPTER 3

"Um...your parrot took my money," I said.

I tried to keep my voice from cracking. I had seen pirates in the movies before but never on the beach. Especially Bondi Beach!

The pirate's un-patched eye twinkled at me. Then he turned to the parrot on his shoulder and growled, "Cecil, yer bildge-sucking bandit! Surrender the loot or prepare to be keel-hauled!"

"Arrrk!" the parrot screeched. He flew onto my shoulder and dropped the bill. I reached out and caught it before it fluttered to the sand.

"Wow," I said, impressed.

"Just a wee trick I taught Cecil here," the pirate said. "The passengers love it."

"Passengers?" I asked as I picked up my money.

The pirate pointed to an old wooden boat docked in a nearby marina. Flapping above the boat was a black and white Jolly Roger flag, with its skull and crossbones.

"Behold the Plunderer's Pride!" the pirate announced. "The finest whale watching ship to sail the briney deep!"

Now I got it. The pirate and his ship were just another whale watching gimmick. So was the money-pecking parrot. But I still wanted to see whales so I had to ask, "How much?"

"For you it's a freebie!" the pirate declared. "To make up for Cecil's scalawaggin ways!"

"Raaaaak!"

Hmm, I thought. *Can I trust this stranger? Is the Plunderer's Pride really a whale-watching boat*?

But when I took another look at the Plunderer's Pride I saw others stepping aboard—a friendly-looking Japanese couple and two gray-haired ladies about the same age as my gran—handing a crewmember their tickets. How could grannies be dangerous?

"Thanks, Mister, Mister—" I said.

"That's Captain to ye!" the pirate snarled. "Captain Nigel Alistair Dread III!"

"Captain Dread! Captain Dread!" Cecil screeched. "Arrrrrk!"

Cecil fluttered off my shoulder and on to the captain's. I followed the pirate and his parrot to the marina and the boat.

So what if it is corny? I thought. *As long as I get to learn about whales!*

I climbed aboard the Plunderer's Pride where I sat between the Japanese couple and the two gray-haired women. They turned out to be sisters from England on holiday.

First Captain Dread introduced us to his "Bondi Buccaneers," Connie and Bruce. They were dressed in pirate getups too—bandanas on their heads, billowy white shirts, and of course, eye-patches! Connie and Bruce gave black eye patches to the other passengers and me and told us to put them on, along with our inflatable life jackets.

"I always wanted to be a pirate!" one of the English ladies said. "Yo, ho, ho!"

Then Bruce stepped into the cabin to start the engine. Soon the Plunderer's Pride was speeding away from Bondi Beach.

"Ahoy me hearties!" Captain Dread declared. "The Plunderer's Pride shall be sailin' down the coast of Australi-arrrrgh! 'Round the isle of Tasmania-arrgh and 'long the shores of Victoria-arrrrgh." He was doing a good job talking like a pirate. But I was more concerned about whales than the route.

"Captain Dread?" I cut in, raising my hand.

The captain stopped mid-introduction. He turned to me and said, "Aye?"

"How many whales do you think we'll see today?" I asked.

Dread stared at me with his uncovered eye. I don't think he was expecting any questions from the passengers!

"Whales?" Dread asked.

"Yeah," I said. "How many whales do you think we'll see on this cruise?"

"Er...heaps of whales," Dread answered.

"Well...how big do whales get?" I asked.

Dread turned to Connie and Bruce. Both mates shook their heads and shrugged.

"Um...very big," Dread said.

"How old does the average whale live to be?" I asked.

"Um...very old," Dread said.

I stared at Captain Dread and his mates. For whale watchers they didn't have a clue about whales. But I refused to give up—even if this was a free ride. I raised my hand to ask another question when Captain Dread shouted, "Belay thy talk, me hearty!"

My mouth clamped shut. I didn't speak pirate, but I had a funny feeling he was telling me to put a sock in it.

Folding my arms I leaned back on the padded bench. "Clueless," I muttered.

But so was I. I didn't know that Cecil the big-beaked parrot was perched right behind me!

"Clueless, clueless, arrrk!" Cecil squawked.

The Japanese couple and English ladies laughed. But Dread glared at me with the steely blue eye I could see. It was enough to shiver me timbers!

What was I thinking going on this crazy cruise? I wondered.

While Dread went on with his pirate act, I stood up and walked to the side of the boat.

Where are the whales? I wondered as I gazed out at the blue ocean. *There have got to be whales out there!*

But all I could see as I walked along the railing was the ocean stretched out for miles. And not a whale in sight!

As I turned to go back to the bench, my foot stubbed something hard. "Ow!" I cried.

Looking down I saw a long rocket-shaped gizmo lying on the deck. It was attached to a coiled up cord. I had never seen anything like that on a boat. Or anywhere!

"Captain Dread, what's this?" I called out.

Captain Dread muttered under his breath as he turned slowly toward me.

"Now what?" he asked.

But when he saw me holding up the silver gizmo his uncovered eye popped wide open.

Uh-oh. I thought. *What did I just do?*

To my surprise—and relief—Dread didn't snap at me. Instead he grabbed Bruce by the collar. He pointed to me holding the gizmo as he shouted, "I told you to pack that thing away after every dive!"

"I-I-I must have forgot!" Bruce stammered.

"You must have kangaroos loose in the paddock, that's what I think!" Dread said, still shouting.

"Thar she blows! Thar she blows!" another shout interrupted the captain. One of the English ladies was pointing far out over the water. The other passengers crowded at the stern and looked across the ocean.

"Ohmigosh!" I gasped as a huge sleek whale

leapt in and out of the water! Dropping the rocket-shaped gizmo I ran to join the others.

Everybody watched the jumping whale. The Japanese woman leaned against the side of the boat while her husband snapped pictures of her and the whale. The English ladies shared a pair of binoculars as they ooh'd and ahh'd. Me, I just stood there—staring out at the most amazing thing I had ever seen since the Great Barrier Reef!

"It's beautiful," I said under my breath.

Is this what the beached baby whale looked like when it was healthy? How many whales like this were left in the sea?

After the whale swam away, the Plunderer's Pride turned and headed back toward shore. I was so busy watching for more whales that I forgot about the creepy Captain Dread and how he treated Bruce. Until we were stepping off the boat and I heard Dread say to Connie and Bruce, "We'd better watch our backs—especially after that beached whale!"

I kept on walking, pretending not to have heard. But my head was spinning with questions...

What do those Bondi Buccaneers know about the beached whale? Did that weird rocket-shaped gizmo I found have anything to do with it?

But as I walked up the beach I saw something else to worry about—my Dad, who was rushing toward me with a concerned look on his face.

"I was looking all over for you, Piper!" Dad exclaimed. "What were you thinking going on a strange boat?"

I gulped. Dad only called me Piper when he was mad. And boy—did he look mad!

CHAPTER 4

"But you said I could go whale-watching, Dad," I told him. "So I could learn more about whales and try to help them!"

Dad looked surprised. "I didn't mean you should just take off on your own!" Dad said. "You should have known better than that, Pip. Going out alone like that could have been dangerous!"

That's for sure! I wanted to tell Dad about creepy Captain Dread and what he said about the beached whale. And the mysterious gizmo. But it would only have made things worse!

And as much as I hate to admit it, Dad was right. Who knows what Dread would have made me do if I had kept asking questions? Make me walk the plank?

But Dad wasn't my biggest problem. When he told Mum what I did, she grounded me big time. That meant no going in the water for a whole day. No big deal to most, but for a serious Surfie like me it was medieval torture!

So the next day I was beached—sitting on the sand and staring out at the ocean I couldn't enjoy.

"I told Dad I couldn't find you, Pip," Elly said. "I hope you're not mad at me."

I ran my hand through the sand, not looking at Elly. Little sisters could have big mouths. But it's not like she was being a lag (tattletale). She was just worried.

"It's okay, El," I sighed. "Go in the water. It's not like you're grounded too."

"Okey-doke!" Elly said, happy to have my permission. She gave a little wave and ran to get her board.

I leaned my chin on my knees as I stared out at the crystal blue water. It seemed like everybody was surfing today—or learning how to. People were swimming and boating too. Even the Plunderer's Pride was drifting on the water. I could see the Bondi Buccaneers in the boat, but no others.

That's weird, I thought. *Why would a whale-watching boat be going out without any whale watchers?*

I was about to stand up for a closer look when I heard someone say, "Hey!"

Looking up I smiled. Standing over me was my BFF, Zara Patakis.

Zara is in the same Mean and Green Club with me at school. Out of all of us Greenies, Zara is the most extreme. She even stopped flushing toilets at home. Her mum isn't too thrilled, but Zara swears she saves heaps of water!

"Hey, Zara!" I said. I was happy to see Zara, not just because I was grounded and wanted company but also because I wanted to tell her all about the beached whale!

"I have to tell you what happened—," I started to say.

"Me first!" Zara cut in. "Guess where I just came

back from? Go ahead—guess!"

"You went to Greece?" I asked. "To visit your grandparents?"

"Nope," Zara said with a shake of her head. "Try again."

I couldn't wait to tell Zara about the beached whale. But I gave it another shot.

"You went to the zoo," I guessed. "To adopt that koala you were talking about."

Zara's eyes lit up when I said that. Lots of wildlife organizations in Australia were letting people "adopt" koalas. For just a few dollars a month, you get a photo and information about your own "adopted" koala and at the same time you can help save the koala population. Zara has had koalas on the brain for a long time!

"As soon as I talk my mum and dad into it, it'll be a go," Zara said. "But guess again."

Now I was getting impatient.

"I'm not psychic, Zara!" I said. "Tell me where you went already!"

"Okay, okay!" Zara said. "We just came back from the Great Barrier Reef!"

I stared at Zara.

Was that a coinky-dink or what?

"Zara, that's where I want to go!" I said. "What

did you do? Spill!"

"Totally awesome," Zara said, plopping down on the sand next to me. "We took a plane there, stayed in a hotel off the reef and snorkeled for two whole days!"

Zara didn't dive like me but as she told me what she saw underneath the water, it didn't seem to make a difference!

"There must have been a thousand different kinds of fish," Zara explained. "Their colors were so bright they looked electric."

"What about the coral?" I asked. "Was it pink and chunky looking? Did it look like a bunch of skeletons?"

Zara shook her head, knowing what I meant. The reef was made up of the skeletons of sea creatures called coral polyps.

"No!" Zara laughed. "They looked more like flowers underwater. After awhile I couldn't tell the coral from the underwater plants!"

I was starting to remember everything about the Great Barrier Reef. How amazing it was—like a paradise under the sea!

"You're so lucky, Zara," I sighed. "I asked my dad if we could go but he can't leave the surf shack."

"Bummer," Zara said. She picked up a fistful

of sand and let the grains pour out between her fingers. "But everything I saw there wasn't so great, you know."

I looked at Zara and asked, "What do you mean?"

"You should have seen all those people trampling all over the reef," Zara said. "I saw one guy knock off a piece of coral and stick it in his pocket as a souvenir! A tee-shirt wasn't enough. He had to bring home a piece of the Great Barrier Reef!"

"Great," I muttered. "By the time I get to the Great Barrier Reef it'll be gone!"

"No it won't," Zara chuckled. "We'll bring it up at our next Mean and Green meeting. Maybe there's something we can do to get the word out."

We high-fived.

Then Zara stood up and nodded toward the ocean. "Let's go in the water," she said. "We'll be back in school before you know it."

"Can't," I said. "I'm grounded."

"Grounded on spring holiday?" Zara gasped. "What did you do—rob a bank?"

Zara listened wide-eyed as I told her about the beached whale and the Bondi Buccaneers.

"Jingoes!" Zara exclaimed. "That Captain Dread sounds as mad as a cut snake. And so are you for sailing out with a lot of creepy pirates. What were you thinking, Pip?"

"I just wanted to learn more about whales so we can protect them," I said. "But I guess my mum is right. I can't save the whole world."

Zara grabbed my arm and pulled to make me stand up. "Then let's do something fun on land," she said. "We can collect rubbish and build a compost pile—right here on the beach!"

"Fun, fun, fun," I giggled as I stood up.

As I brushed sand from my legs I looked out at the water one last time. I could see a boy bobbing up and down in the waves flapping both his arms. I looked around to see who he was waving to.

When I didn't see anyone, it clicked. The boy wasn't waving—he was drowning!

In a flash, my Nipper instincts kicked in. Grounded or not, I raced to the water to save the drowning kid.

"I thought you couldn't go in the ocean!" Zara shouted.

I ignored my friend as I charged ahead. Standing on the beach was Elly holding her shortboard. She yelped as I yanked it out from under her arm.

"What are you doing, Pip?" Elly complained. "You're not supposed to go in the water anyway.

You're grounded!"

Yeah, I knew, I knew. But being grounded was the last thing on my mind as I jumped on the board and paddled toward the drowning boy.

"Hold on!" I shouted out. "I'm coming!"

CHAPTER 5

The boy was just going under as I paddled over. I reached down and grabbed his arm. As I pulled him above the water I shouted, "Grab the board! Grab the board!"

"Okay," he gasped as he grabbed onto the side of my surfboard.

I jumped off my board and shoved him up on it. Then I popped up and paddled us both safely to the shore.

"I'm Pip," I said. "What's your name?"

"William," he answered, out of breath. "Will Carmichael."

"Hey, Will," I said with a smile. "No worries. You're safe now."

When we reached shallow water, we both climbed off the board. Will looked about eleven years old, just like me. His hair was ginger-colored and he was wearing denim board shorts.

"I must have gotten caught in the rip, Pip," Will said. "I guess I owe you one."

"I'm a Nipper," I said. "It's our job to save people. Or at least to learn how."

"Well done, mate!" Will said. He clapped me on the back. "You saved my life!"

Those four little words hit me like a ton of conch shells. I had always wanted to save someone and I just did!

"Rah, Pipper!" a voice cheered. I turned toward the beach. Zac was grinning and giving me a thumbs-up sign. Others were clapping and smiling at me—like Zara and Elly!

"That's my sister!" Elly said, pointing to me and jumping up and down. "And that was my board!"

I couldn't believe it. I was a hero! But when I saw my dad, I remembered that I was a hero who broke the rules.

"I didn't mean to go in the water, Dad," I said. "But when I saw Will drowning—"

"You don't have to explain, Pip," Dad said. "I'm very proud of you."

It was totally weird to go from zero to hero in just minutes. But it felt great!

Dad turned to Will and asked, "Is your mum or dad around?"

"No," Will said. "But here comes my gran."

I turned to see where Will was pointing. Stumbling across the sand on high heeled sandals was a tall woman wearing a huge brimmed hat. Her lemon-yellow trouser suit seemed out of place on the beach. As she got closer, I saw what was inside her gold tote bag—a teacup Chihuahua dog!

"Will, my darling!" the woman cried. "When Gran saw you drowning, her heart went pit-a-pat, pit-a-pat!"

"I'm okay, Gran," Will said. He blushed as his grandmother kissed him all over his face. "This girl saved me. Her name's Pip."

Will's gran looked over her gigantic sunnies at me. "Yes, I saw!" she said. "And such a heroic feat calls for a little reward!"

"Pip, you're going to be rich!" Elly squeaked. I clapped my hand over Elly's mouth.

"Oh, Pip can't accept any reward," Dad said for me. "She's a Nipper and it's part of her job."

"I wasn't thinking about money," Will's gran said. She flashed a big grin and announced, "I am Madame Vera-Victoria."

"Uh-huh," I said, nodding politely. But the woman locked her gaze on me. As if she expected a huge reaction.

"Madame Vera-Victoria," she repeated. "Of the Aussie Glossie Spa?"

That name I knew. The Aussie Glossie Spa was right down the street from my mum's travel agency in Sydney. It was in a gold-painted building behind a big black fence. I must have passed it a million times.

"I know the Aussie Glossie Spa," I said with a nod.

"I knew you would!" Madame Vera-Victoria said.

The Chihuahua growled as Madame reached into the tote bag and pulled out two envelopes. "I would like to give you two free passes to my spa," she said. "For saving my precious Will."

"Gran," Will groaned, blushing.

I stared at the envelopes in Madame Vera-Victoria's hand. The only thing I knew about spas were from the telly (TV). They were places where women went to get their toenails painted and their

43

faces slopped with seaweed mush.

"Thanks," I said. "But I'm only eleven—"

"We have a fabulous spa package for little girls!" Madame Vera-Victoria declared. "How does a peanut butter facial and hot chocolate foot soak sound to you?"

Truth, it sounded gross. But instead I nodded politely and said, "Very...nice."

"Right!" Madame Vera-Victoria said. She handed me the two envelopes. "There you are—one pass for you and one pass for your friend."

"Excuse me?" Zara asked. "Didn't your spa once use whale blubber in their cosmetics and creams?"

Madame Vera-Victoria narrowed her eyes at Zara. Then she snatched one of the envelopes out of my hand and said, "Actually…why don't you come alone and make new friends?"

"Thank you, Madame Victoria-Vera," I said.

"That's Vera-Victoria," she said a bit annoyed. "See you at the spa. And hooroo (goodbye)!"

Will waved to me as he followed his gran up the beach. I waved back. Will seemed like a nice kid— even if his gran was a bit of a fruit loop!

"Well, Pip," Dad said with a smile. "That was very nice of Madame Vera-Victoria!"

But Zara wasn't smiling. "Are you really going to go to that silly spa?" she asked. "What if they still use whale blubber cream?"

"She said they use peanut butter," I shrugged.

"Ew!" Elly said. "I'd rather eat it than put it on my face!"

Me too. But Dad was right. It was nice of Madame Vera-Victoria to give me something. But even better was that I finally got to save a life!

I spent the next hour or so helping Dad wax surfboards. I was a hero, but still a grounded one. As I waxed a board with a cool whale design, it made me think of the beached baby beluga yesterday.

45

Maybe it won't happen again, I thought. *Maybe it was just a fluke.* I giggled at the pun. A fluke is a whale's tail!

By tea time I was back in my house watching Mum plan trips in her home office: A picture-taking safari in Africa for a honeymooning couple. A trip to Bali for an Australian family. A trip to Scandanavia for a college professor.

All those great trips for everyone—except us Whelans!

"It's great that you saved that boy, Pip," Mum said.

I looked over Mum's shoulder as she researched hotels in Sweden. One hotel was made totally out of ice.

"I guess my Nipper training paid off," I said.

"Your dad was a Nipper too," Mum said smiling up at me. "Swimming seems to be in the Whelan blood."

"I think I know why," I said.

"Why?" Mum asked as she scrolled up the page.

"Because Benjamin Whelan's convict ship sank off the coast of Australia!" I said. "So Benjamin and the other passengers had to swim all the way to shore!"

"Mm-hm," Mum said as if she'd heard the story

a million times. But I never got tired of telling it.

"They never found the ship but it was called the HMS Primrose," I went on. "Such a nice name for such a sad ship, don't you think?"

"Mm-hm," Mum said, paying more attention to the screen than to me.

"Anyway," I said. "That's how the Whelan water-connection all started."

"If you say so!" Mum said as she stared at the computer screen. "Oh—this hotel has a great deal. And it's five stars!"

I wrapped my arms around Mum's neck. Now that she was a travel agent, I thought I'd try my luck…

"How about a hero's celebration, Mum?" I asked. "And I happen to know the perfect place."

"Your favorite Indian restaurant?" Mum asked. "We had take-away chicken curry yesterday."

"Not a restaurant, Mum," I said. "The Great Barrier Reef!"

"You were there when you were seven," Mum said.

"I know, but it may not be there for long," I said. "Zara says the surface is already starting to wear out. Because of all the tourists tramping over it."

"Those tourists happen to be putting food in our mouths," Mum said. "At your dad's surf shack and my travel agency."

"I know," I said, feeling heaps guilty.

"Speaking of food," Mum said, standing up. "I was planning to cook the hero her favorite dish tonight."

"Lasagna?" I gasped. I kissed my fingers and declared, "Molta bene!"

"I thought that would cheer you up!" Mum said with a grin.

After Mum left the room, I sat in front of the computer. But just as I was about to do a search on whales I got an IM from Zara:

RU There? JFI – Dolphin beached at Bondi 2Day. G2G.

My mouth fell open as I stared at the screen. This time it wasn't a whale that was beached.

It was a *dolphin!*

CHAPTER 6

The news about the beached dolphin must have had an extreme effect on my appetite because I ate two servings of my mum's lasagna instead of my usual three.

How did the dolphin become beached? Did the Bondi Buccaneers have anything to do with it? There was just one way to find out...

"Can I go to the beach extra-early tomorrow?" I asked. "So I can find out more about that dolphin."

"Can I help?" Elly asked.

"I have a better idea, Pip," Mum said, wiping sauce off of Elly's chin. "Why don't you go to the Aussie Glossie Spa tomorrow?"

"The Aussie Glossie?" I cried.

"If you ask me, you could use a little pampering," Mum said calmly.

"Your Mum is right," Dad said. "All this talk about dead whales and dolphins can't be very healthy."

"They're not dead, Dad," I said. "But they might be if we don't do something to help them."

"Pip," Mum said. "You know you can't save—"

"—the whole world," I finished. "I know, I know."

I could have begged until all my teeth fell out. But Mum insisted on taking me to the Aussie Glossie Spa.

So as the sun came up over Sydney the next morning, Mum and I headed to the city for a whole day of slathering and soaking!

Before going to the Aussie Glossie, Mum and I had brekkie in an outdoor café. I ate a yummy cranberry scone while Mum had rock melon (cantaloupe) and espresso. From where we sat I could see the Sydney Opera House with its towering arches looming over the harbor. Next to it was a fun park. And nearby was the Sydney Aquarium.

"Can we go to the Aquarium, Mum?" I asked. "There's got to be some stuff about whales and dolphins there."

"No, Pip," Mum sighed over her espresso.

I should have known Mum wouldn't have agreed to the aquarium. So I tried the selfless approach...

"Mum, how about if we go to Chinatown instead of the spa?" I asked. "You can buy that awesome blue silk jacket you had your eye on. You would look so great in that silk jacket!"

"Nice try, Pip," Mum said. "But I already made a reservation for you at the Aussie Glossie."

So off to the spa we went.

"Good morning!" a woman wearing a white coat chirped as she opened the door. "And you are?"

"This is Piper Whelan," Mum said. "She has a pass—"

"I know exactly who you are!" the woman said. "Would you like a cup of green tea? Some soy crisps (chips)?"

"No, thank you," I said.

"Then I'll get Madame!" the woman declared.

Mum and I stood in the entrance hall. Gold starfish were stenciled on soft blue walls. Piped in was some kind of New Age music that sounded like wind chimes. I was actually starting to relax until—

"Ah! There's my little Kipper!"

I whipped around at the shrill sound of Madame Vera-Victoria's voice. There she was, coming down a sweeping staircase dressed in a black dress and silver sandals. She was holding a coffee mug with the words "Boss Lady" written across it.

I took a whiff. What she was drinking smelled a lot more like strong coffee than green tea!

"Um…it's Nipper," I said. "I'm a Nipper."

"Of course!" Madame said. She took a sip of coffee, leaving a red lippie (lipstick) mark on the rim. Then she turned to Mum. "Mrs. Whelan, I would like to take Pip to our Pampered Princess Parlour. Would you like a treatment too while you wait for her?"

"Oh, I'd love one," Mum said. "But I have to work."

"What a shame!" Madame said, not looking too disappointed.

Just then the door swung open and a man stepped inside. He was wearing a khaki shirt and faded jeans. His face was covered with beard stubble and he had a huge canvas sack slung over his shoulder.

"G'day," he said in a gruff voice. "I'm here for my…um…mani-pedi."

Madame took one look at the ciggy hanging from

the corner of his mouth and frowned.

"Sir," Madame said. "The Aussie Glossie is a smoke-free establishment."

The man blinked as he yanked out his ciggy. Then he stubbed it out in the pebbles of a lucky bamboo plant!

Madame rolled her eyes to the ceiling then turned back to me. "Say goodbye to your mum, princess," she said. "Then Laura will spirit you away for your royal treatment!"

"Bye, Pip," Mum said, giving me a peck on the cheek. "Enjoy yourself."

Before I could say goodbye, Laura whisked me inside the changing room. There I kicked off my uggies (boots) and hung my clothes and pouch in my own locker. I wrapped myself in a fluffy pink robe and slipped my feet into fuzzy slippers.

"Ready?" Laura asked with a smile.

"Ready," I sighed.

With a wave of her hand, Laura led me into an eye-popping room that looked like the inside of a genie's bottle!

The walls were painted pink and the ceiling was purple with gold stars. There were heaps of gold pillows thrown all over the floor and sheer gold curtains over the windows.

Women wearing short dresses and glittery wings tried not to trip over the pillows as they carried bowls of creams and bottles of lotions.

I glanced at a row of pink chairs against one wall. Sitting in them were more pampered princesses. One girl had cucumbers stuck over her eyes. Another was getting her toenails painted blue. But when I saw the girls in the last two chairs I wanted to bolt! They were Lucy and Darcy—the twins who were grossed out by the beached whale two days ago.

Lucy had some bright green cream on her face that looked like pea soup. Darcy had lemon slices stuck between her toes while they were being polished sparkly silver.

"Isn't that the girl from the beach the other day?" Lucy whispered loud enough for me to hear.

"She didn't look like the spa type," Darcy whispered back. "More the sporty type if you ask me."

As I waved to the twins, a woman wearing a purple velvet dress and fairy wings stepped in front of me.

"Cheers!" she said. "I'm your Fairy-in-Waiting Fiona! Are you ready for a princess-perfect facial?"

"Bring it," I said with a shrug.

Fairy Fiona seated me in a chair next to a sink. She pulled a lever and the chair tilted all the way back—like at the dentist's!

"Would you like peanut butter to draw out the impurities?" Fairy Fiona asked. "Or vanilla frosting to soften and moisturize?"

"How about Vegemite?" I joked. "This is the land of Oz, you know."

The girl in the chair next to me gasped.

"Did you say the land of Oz?" she asked. "Like in Dorothy and Toto and the Wizard?"

I gave the girl a sideways glance. She looked about Elly's age, and from her accent I could tell she was from America.

"Australia is sometimes called Oz," I explained. "You know as in *Oz*-tralia!"

"Oh!" the girl said. "Cool!"

"And Vegemite," I went on, "is an Australian vegetable spread that's been around for ages—"

Splat! I gasped as a huge glob of peanut butter landed smack on my forehead. I'm not grossed out easily but I felt myself gag as Fairy Fiona spread peanut butter over my face with a wooden stick. I tried to take my mind off of it by thinking about my favorite place in the world—the beach. But once I thought about the beach, I thought about the whale and the dolphin!

Why were there two beached mammals in a row? Why was Captain Dread so mad when I found that strange rocket-shaped thingy? Did it have anything to do with the whale or the dolphin?

"Done!" Fairy Fiona declared. "And now your highness, thy throne awaits!"

She tilted my chair up so fast I almost catapulted across the room. As I walked toward Lucy and Darcy I smiled and said, "Hi." Not that I wanted to chat, but I didn't want them to think I was snooty either.

"Is this place heaps of fun or what?" Lucy asked me. "We come here at least once a week."

"Once a week?" I asked.

Darcy wiggled her toes and said, "How else are we going to get gross sand out from under our toenails?"

I giggled to myself as I decided to have some fun. "I don't know much about toenails, mates," I said. "I bite mine down to the quick!"

"You...bite...your...toenails?" Darcy asked.

"You know us *sporty* girls," I answered with a smile. "We can't be bothered with scissors." No way did I bite my toenails—ever! But it was fun seeing the twins' grossed out faces! And it did the trick. The earbashing stopped. But it didn't stop the sticky peanut butter from feeling stickier and stickier!

I don't care if it is part of my pampered princess package! I thought. *I'm washing this goop off!*

"Pardon," I said. "May I take a dunny (bathroom) break?"

Fairy Fiona looked up from sticking kiwi slices between my toes. "Of course," she said. "You'll find the dunny down the hall right past Madame's office."

It was hard walking with kiwi between my toes, but I hobbled my way out of the Pampered Princess Parlour. Halfway down the hall, I heard Madame's voice booming out of her office. "That's my offer. You can take it or leave it."

"Deal!" a gruff voice said.

"Good!" Madame said. "Now go hit the frog 'n toad (hit the road) so I can get back to work."

I was about to take a step when someone shot out of Madame's office. It was the man with the canvas sack. But this time his sack was empty.

What was in it? I wondered. I glanced down at his grimy feet in pluggers (flip-flops). *And what happened to the pedicure he came for?*

Suddenly I heard Madame's voice again:

"Don't give me that rubbish!…You heard what I said…That's a lame excuse if I ever heard one!" This time it sounded like she was yelling at someone over the phone. "I want more convict stuff…You know, like chains and shackles!"

My jaw dropped. Chains? Shackles? What did posh Madame Vera-Victoria need chains and shackles for?

Unless, I thought with a gulp. *It's to keep princesses like me from leaving their thrones!*

CHAPTER 7

"Forget the dunny," I whispered, too scared to pass Madame Vera-Victoria's office. But just as I was about to head back to the Pampered Princess Parlour I felt something cold and wet nibbling on my foot.

Glancing down I saw Madame's tiny teacup Chihuahua. The little dog was chewing the kiwi slices between my toes!

I was about to shake the little ankle-biter off my foot when a voice shouted, "Genghis!"

The little Chihuahua looked up and whined. Then it scampered away from my foot and into Madame's office.

"Genghis, what's wrong, baby?" Madame's voice cooed. Her door slammed shut and I whirled around. Standing behind me with his mouth wide open was Will!

"Aaaaaa!" Will screamed when he saw me.

"Aaaaaa!" I screamed back. I'm usually not a screamer, but Will's yelling spooked me. Suddenly I remembered my yucky face mask. The poor guy

probably thought I was some kind of bog-monster!

"Will, it's me, Pip," I said, licking peanut butter off my lips. "This stuff is peanut butter!"

"It's only peanut butter…it's only peanut butter…," Will kept repeating as he tried to calm down.

"What are you doing here, Will?" I asked. "Do you live in the spa with your grandmother?"

"No, thank goodness!" Will said. "I'm just staying with Gran while my mum and dad holiday in Europe."

"Oh," I said. "Sorry to scare you like that."

"Me? Scared?" Will said with a laugh. "I knew it was you all the time!"

Yeah, right.

"My gran told me you were coming," Will said. He flashed a big smile. "So I wanted to give you a prezzie (present) for saving my life!"

"Really?" I asked. I loved prezzies!

"It's a surprise!" Will said excitedly. "Close your eyes and hold out your hand."

My eyelids felt sticky as I squeezed my eyes shut. I could feel something cold and round being placed in my palm.

"Open them!" Will said.

Glancing down I saw something that looked like an antique watch. But instead of two hands it had one needle moving slightly.

"What is it?" I asked.

"It's an ancient compass," Will explained. "Sailors used it to see which direction their ship was going in—north, south, east or west."

I watched the needle move as I stepped in four different directions. East, north, south and west.

For something ancient it worked like a champ!

"Thanks, Will," I said. "Where did you get it?"

"Can't tell you," Will said, shaking his head. "My gran made me promise not to."

"Why'd she do that?" I asked.

"I'm not allowed to talk about a lot of stuff I see around this place," Will sighed. "And speaking of secrets, don't let my gran know I gave you the compass. If she finds out she'll flip!"

She already has, I thought. But I dropped the compass into the pocket of my robe and said, "My lips are zipped."

"Oh, Pip!" a voice called sweetly.

I glanced past Will's shoulder. Fairy Fiona was standing at the end of the hall. "Would you like mini-marshmallows in your hot chocolate foot soak?" she asked. "Or whipped cream?"

I looked at Will as if to say, "Help me!

"Good luck," Will whispered.

I followed the fairy back into the pink, sugary-smelling room. But as I sat down and sank my feet into a tub of hot chocolate, my head was spinning with questions. What was in that guy's bag? Why was Madame talking on the phone about chains and shackles? And most of all—What's such a big secret about a tarnished old compass?

After another hour or so my perfect-princess treatments were finally over. The peanut butter was washed off my face and my feet felt chocolaty smooth.

I had to admit that it was kind of fun. Especially when Fairy Fiona painted my toenails—green, of course! When Mum picked me, up she swore I was a new girl!

"I knew this spa would be a good idea," Mum said. "It makes me want to be pampered too!"

"And so you shall!" I said, waving my new magic wand filled with bath powder. All pampered princesses got one for coming to the spa.

Madame Vera-Victoria came to the door to say goodbye. When she looked down at my feet she frowned. "You stuffed your princess-perfect pedicure into boots?" Madame gasped.

"They're my uggies!" I said, picking up one foot. "Wherever I go, they go."

"I see," Madame said, pursing her lips.

As Mum and I turned to the door a tall bearded man walked inside.

"Can I help you?" Madame asked.

"Yeah!" the man said with a wink. "I'm here for my...you know...olive oil and apricot beauty scrub."

I raised an eyebrow when I saw the bloke's arms covered with snake tattoos. *And they say I'm not the spa type!* I thought.

"Of course, Bruno!" Madame told the man. She then smiled at Mum and me and waved us out the door. "I hope you'll both come back soon. Hooroo!"

"Hooroo and thanks!" Mum said as we left the spa.

I smiled to myself and opened the gate. Pampering over, now I could finally get down to business—the business of beached whales and dolphins!

Mum and I took the bus home. Then I went straight to the beach to find Zac and ask him about the dolphin.

"Did you eat a peanut butter sandwich today, Pip?" Zac asked, sniffing the air.

"It's a long story, Zac," I sighed. "But did you hear about the beached dolphin yesterday?"

"I sure did," Zac said.

"Any news?" I asked.

"Sorry, Pipper," Zac said. "The dolphin died before he got to the wildlife hospital."

Ouch! I felt like I was kicked in the stomach.

"How did it happen, Zac?" I asked.

"It could be a number of reasons," Zac said. "More mammals are being beached because of global warming and the changing depth of the ocean." I got that. We talked about global warming in our Mean and Green meetings. "Then there's sonar equipment," Zac went on.

"Sonar equipment?" I asked. "What's that?"

"Divers often use side scan sonar to study the ocean floor," Zac explained. "They hang it from their boats and use its sound waves to search the water. The device displays images on a screen of what's down below."

"If it's just sound," I said. "How can it be dangerous to whales and dolphins?"

"Done right, sonar devices can be very helpful," Zac said. "But high frequencies can confuse whales or dolphins, making them swim into shallow waters where they get beached."

I remembered that weird-looking gizmo I found attached to the Plunderer's Pride. Was that a sonar device? If it was, what were Captain Dread and his crew using one for?

I gazed at the Plunderer's Pride docked in the marina. There was only one way to find out!

CHAPTER 8

"Avast, me bonny buccaneers," I whispered as I made my way across the beach to the marina. "Prepare ye for doom!"

I stopped when I saw Captain Dread, Bruce and Connie in the distance. All three were on the beach talking to visitors.

Probably trying to sign up passengers, I thought.

With the pirates busy, the coast was clear. I would sneak onto the Plunderer's Pride and see if the gizmo was still on deck. Then I'd check for any labels reading side scan sonar.

With one eye out for the pirates, I raced down the dock toward the Plunderer's Pride. As I jumped onto the deck the boat swayed softly. Sort of like my surfboard on a gentle wave.

"Okay," I told myself. "Where is it?"

The rocket-shaped gizmo was not where I found it the other day. Instead I found a huge blue plastic trunk!

Could it be in there? I wondered.

Lifting the lid I peered inside. The trunk was

filled with diving gear —wetsuits, masks and flippers.

Suddenly I heard voices. It sounded like Captain Dread and his mates!

I knew I had to hide— but where?

Quickly I ducked behind the trunk. That's when I saw it—the silver rocket-shaped gizmo and a flat black box that looked like a computer. Was it the screen Zac was talking about?

I was about to pick it up when I heard a voice growl, "Looking for something, lassie?"

Gulp. My blood ran ice-cold. I knew that voice. It was Captain Dread's!

"G'day," I said as I slipped out from behind the trunk. "I must have dropped my Nipper badge the other day. By any chance, did you find it?"

Cecil fluttered onto Dread's shoulder. Connie and Bruce walked over. I could tell by their smirky looks that they didn't buy my lost-badge story.

"The kid was snooping, Nigel," Connie said.

"What were you looking for?" Bruce demanded.

I gathered my guts and said, "I told you—my Nipper badge!"

Captain Dread stepped right up to me. As he leaned over I could feel his hot breath on my face. "Dead men tell no tales," he snarled. "If me or my mates catch you on this boat again, you'll be snooping around in Davy Jones' Locker!"

My eyes popped wide open. Davy Jones' Locker meant the bottom of the ocean!

"Davy Jones! Davy Jones!" Cecil screeched. "Raaak!"

Connie and Bruce laughed but I didn't think it was funny. There was something sinister about those pirate wannabes. And I was pretty sure that rocket-shaped gizmo was a side scan sonar too!

"I really hate to pike out but I have to be home in time for dinner," I said. "Ahoy, mates!"

I slipped past the pirates and high-tailed it off the Plunderer's Pride.

"Whew!" I gasped as I hurried up the beach. "That was close!"

If only I had gotten a better look at the rocket-shaped gizmo and the black box. But I had seen enough.

Everything about it spelled side scan sonar to me.

But what were the Bondi Buccaneers using one for?

To search underwater for whales? I wondered. Then I shook my head. If that's all it was, why did Captain Dread flip when I found it?

This is a mystery, I decided. *But I'm going to solve it if it's the last thing I ever do!*

And with those creepy pirates on my heels, it might just be!

After my scary encounter with Captain Dread, I was happy to make it home in one piece. Mum had brought home Chinese take-away food. So we all sat around the table eating with chopsticks—or in Elly's case, trying to!

"Elly," I said. "You're supposed to put the food in your mouth, not on your lap."

Elly stuck her chin out and said, "Practice makes perfect, you know!" She balanced another mushroom on two chopsticks then popped it into her mouth. "See?" she said after gulping it down.

"Yay, you!" Dad cheered.

I was happy too. Now we could get back to talking about the Bondi Buccaneers. I had told Mum and Dad about the sonar device I found on the Plunderer's Pride. What I didn't tell them was that I was on the boat a second time!

"Why would the pirates be using a side scan sonar

device in the first place?" I said, after sipping some jasmine tea.

"If they're pirates," Elly giggled. "Maybe they're searching for buried treasure!"

"Can we be serious?" I asked.

"There's nothing wrong with using side scan sonars, Pip," Dad said. "As long as they use it the right way and for the right reasons."

"I know, Dad, but—" I started to say.

"Pip," Mum cut in, "Your Dad has something to tell you and Elly."

I had a funny feeling Mum was trying to change the subject. "What is it?" I sighed.

Dad's eyes twinkled as he said, "We are going to the Great Barrier Reef for a few days. I've decided to take some time off after all."

The Great Barrier Reef?

Elly gave a little gasp. All I could do was stare at Dad before finally saying, "Fair dinkum?" (truth)

"Fair dinkum!" Dad said with a nod.

"Thanks, Dad!" I squealed.

"Don't thank me. Thank your mum," Dad said.

"I was able to work something out with a hotel I do business with," Mum said. "And I get a discount on airfare so it's all set."

"Are we all going?" Elly asked, bouncing up and

down on her chair.

"Not me, I'm afraid," Mum said. "I just started my job, so I can't take a holiday quite yet."

"But I sure can use a holiday," Dad said. "So it won't kill me to close the shack for a couple of days."

I was so excited I could do cartwheels around the kitchen. I would go diving and see millions of fish and plants and coolest of all, the Great Barrier Reef!

Elly grabbed her water glass and began blowing bubbles through her straw.

"What are you doing?" I asked.

"Practicing my snorkeling!" Elly said. She was too young to go diving. But I wasn't. I already had my diving certificate from taking scuba lessons at the local pool. So everything was all systems go!

"The Great Barrier Reef is over two thousand kilometers away," Dad said. "We'll stay on Lizard Island…"

Dad's voice trailed off as I pictured myself diving under the crystal clear waters. I couldn't wait to go! Until I realized something that made my stomach do a triple flip. *If I'm going to be thousands of kilometers away, who's going to save the whales and the dolphins?*

t wasn't easy, but I decided not to think about whales, dolphins or pirates for the next two days.

I studied up on Lizard Island even though it was spring holiday and there was no school. It was worth it, because the stuff I found out was totally neat.

Like, I never knew Lizard Island was the most northern island in the Great Barrier Reef. And that long ago it was called Dyiigurra by the Aboriginal people who thought of it as a sacred place.

It was Captain Cook, the famous sea captain of the 1700's, who named it Lizard Island because all he could see there were lizards. Maybe the captain wasn't looking hard enough, because the Aboriginal people used the island to harvest fish, shellfish and turtles!

Anyway, feeling like an expert on the Great Barrier Reef and Lizard Island, I finally took off with Dad and Elly for the holiday of my life.

"How does this thing work?" Elly asked as we

sat on the plane. She was fumbling with our new underwater camera on her lap.

"Easy," I said. "You just point it at a shark and click!"

"Shark?" Elly squeaked. "Are we really going to swim with sharks?"

"Just joshin'!" I said before Dad could jump in.

I was just joshin'. As much as I loved all kinds of wildlife I didn't want to get up close and personal with sharks!

"Hey," I said, looking out the window of the plane. "Did you know that the Great Barrier Reef can be seen from outer space?"

"Really?" Dad said, his eyes glued to his surfing magazine.

"And that it's one of the wonders of the world?" I asked. "Along with the Taj Mahal in India, the Grand Canyon in America, Mount Everest in Tibet—"

"Really?" Dad said with his eyes still on his magazine.

I figured my next little factoid would get his attention for sure. "And did you know that there are some ants on Lizard Island that taste like oranges?" I asked.

"Eww!" Elly cried.

"Pip!" Dad said, looking up from his magazine. "Is that another one of your jokes?"

"No!" I said, shaking my head. "It's what I found out doing research!"

"I'll eat brussel sprouts, cabbage and spinach," Elly said. "But no way am I eating ants!"

We finally arrived at the Lizard Island Airport. A taxi took us to our resort which was right on a sandy white beach. Dad checked us in and then we checked out our room. I wasn't too thrilled to have to share a bed with Elly. The thought of her snoring in my ear like a mozzie (mosquito) didn't thrill me either, but when I looked out the window our view did.

"There's the Great Barrier Reef!" I exclaimed. "I'm putting on my wetsuit right now!"

"Not so fast," Dad said. "We won't fly and dive on the same day. We'll wait until tomorrow." Dad said.

Sure, I was disappointed. But there were heaps of other stuff to do on Lizard Island. So after buying sangers (sandwiches) and chips (fries) at a stand on the beach we took a boat to Osprey Island to see nesting sea birds.

Later Dad, Elly and I took a hike to the top of Cook's Lookout for an awesome view of the ocean.

"When did Captain Cook sail to Australia?" Elly

asked as we gazed out at the sapphire-blue waters.

After all my research I knew the answer to that.

"Sometime in the 1700's," I said. "Around the same time Benjamin Whelan sailed to Australia from Ireland."

"Do you think Benjamin Whelan met Captain Cook?" Elly asked.

"Who knows? Nobody's even sure what happened to his ship!" I said, my eyes still on the ocean.

What if the HMS Primrose crashed into the Great Barrier Reef and sunk somewhere out there?

That night I was so deadbeat (tired) from all that traveling and sightseeing I fell asleep before I could hear Elly snore!

When my eyes popped open the next morning I practically jumped out of bed and into my wetsuit. I was going to dive the Great Barrier Reef at last!

Dad, Elly and I ate a good brekki of eggs and snags (sausages). Then we joined a diving boat that would take us out in the ocean. Our skipper, Gillian, introduced us to the dive-master, Colin, whose shiny black wetsuit made him look like a seal! The plan was that Dad would go snorkeling with Elly while I went diving with Colin and some other guests.

I was wearing a new blue tiger-print wetsuit and feeling really cool. I also wore the underwater camera around my neck so I hoped those fish were ready for their close-ups!

Gillian drove the cabin cruiser to what seemed like the middle of the ocean. The last boat I had been on was the Plunderer's Pride—but I tried not to think about that!

When the boat stopped, Gillian dropped anchor. The snorkelers began pulling on their masks. We divers put on our own masks, plus tanks and flippers.

Colin double-checked my gear. Then came the moment I was waiting for—the big dive!

I sat on the edge of the boat then fell backward into the water with a splash. Tiny bubbles floated and popped around me as I breathed through my regulator. As I looked through my mask, I couldn't believe my eyes. Fish in all colors, shapes and sizes were swimming by me as if I was one of them. Even a giant sea turtle flapped by!

Awesome! I said to myself. The coral wasn't just coral-colored. It was green, blue, yellow and white! And like Zara said, they really did look like flowers!

I felt like the Little Mermaid as I snapped

pictures of clown fish, angel fish and blue green puller fish that sparkled like turquoise stones.

No wonder the Great Barrier Reef was one of the Wonders of the World. And if it could be seen from outer space, what were the Martians waiting for? Everybody into the water!

By the time I swam up to our boat, I was as happy as a clam. And as our boat drifted back to the beach, Dad, Elly and I couldn't stop sharing fish stories.

"Can we go diving again tomorrow, Dad?" I asked as we stepped on the beach.

"We have to go home tomorrow, Pip," Dad said.

My heart sank. How could I leave all this? While Dad and Elly headed for the hotel, I lagged behind. I stopped to check out something on the sand that looked like a giant crab!

"G'day, Mister Crab!" I told it. I normally don't talk to sea creatures, but my diving trip had me feeling close to nature! "You remind me of a joke," I went on. "A guy goes into a restaurant and asks, 'Do you serve crabs here?' So the waiter says, 'We serve everybody—have a seat!'"

The creature began scurrying away.

I guess he doesn't like crab jokes.

I was about to catch up with Dad and Elly when

I took one last look at the ocean. A guy was hobbling out of the water holding onto his leg. As I looked closer I saw that his leg was cut up and bleeding!

"Hello?" I called. "Are you okay?"

"Yeah…yeah," the man gasped as his leg dripped red blood on the white sand. "I'm fine."

But my Nipper instincts told me he needed first aid. And fast!

"How did you cut yourself?" I asked the man as I ran over to him. "What happened?"

The man gritted his teeth. I couldn't tell whether he was in pain or whether he was mad at me.

"I was attacked," he blurted. "By a shark!"

I froze in my tracks. Did he say, "Shark?"

My hands flew up to my mouth. I turned to the ocean and began to scream, "Shark! Shark! Everybody out of the water!"

CHAPTER 10

I must have yelled pretty loud because in a flash swimmers and snorkelers came running out of the water. Charging toward the ocean were three surf lifesavers!

"That man is hurt!" I told one. "A shark bit his leg and he's bleeding like a stuck pig!"

A crowd of people from the resort had gathered onto the beach. Dad and Elly ran next to me just as the water police zoomed over on their boat.

"Are you okay, Pip?" Dad asked. He put his arm around my shoulder and squeezed.

"I'm fine, Dad!" I said. "No worries."

More swimmers and snorkelers raced out of the water. One mum was holding her baby under her arm. Another man still had his snorkel mask on.

"Look at all the people you saved, Pip," Elly said proudly. "You're a hero all over again!"

Some people were screaming as they ran out of the water and up the beach. "Somebody saw a shark!" and "Don't go in the water!"

It was pure chaos. But the important thing was

that everybody was safe from the shark—wherever it was.

Two police officers, a man and a woman, stepped out of their boat and walked up the beach.

"Okay," the tall policeman said, his mustache dancing above his lip. "Who saw the shark?"

I glanced back at the wounded man. He didn't raise his hand. Instead he was trying to hobble away.

"He saw it!" I said, pointing at the guy. "He was bitten by a shark and needs help!"

The man froze on the sand.

"Where'd you see the shark, mate?" the policeman called.

The man stared back at the officers like a deer in headlights. "Um," he said. "In the water?"

After eyeballing the guy, the policeman muttered to his partner. "I don't think he saw a shark, Lindy."

"Doesn't look like it," Officer Lindy agreed.

Elly turned to me with wide eyes. "That man didn't see a shark, Pip," she said. "You saved all those people for nothing!"

"But he said—" I started to say.

"Pip," Dad said in a low voice, "You shouldn't shout 'shark' unless you're absolutely sure. Look at all the panic you caused on the beach."

"But I was sure, Dad!" I said. "That guy told me he was bitten by a shark. I heard it with my own two ears!"

But what if my own two ears were clogged with water from all that diving? What if I heard the guy all wrong? Suddenly I felt pretty dumb. "I was only trying to help, Dad," I sighed.

"I know," Dad said with a nod. "But go apologize to the police. It's the right thing to do."

"Okay," I said. I took a deep breath and walked over to the officers. The policeman was still watching the man as a lifesaver tended his leg.

"Excuse me, officer," I started to say.

But the two officers were busy talking to each other.

"Hey, Lindy," the policeman was saying. "I think I know that guy from somewhere."

"Where, Al?" Officer Lindy asked.

"Watch," Al said, leading Officer Lindy in the direction of the bleeding man. I was curious so I went too.

"So, mate," Officer Al told the man, "How's the leg coming along?"

"My leg?" the man asked. His voice cracked as if he was more scared than hurt. "Um…"

When the man didn't answer the lifesaver said, "He's got heaps of wooden splinters in the wound."

"Splinters, eh?" Officer Al said. "Was the shark that attacked you chewing on a toothpick?"

"Maybe...maybe not," the man said in a cheeky way.

Officer Al's mustache began to twitch. And even though he was wearing dark sunnies I could see his eyes starting to narrow.

"Rubbish!" Officer Al snapped. "You got those splinters from looting a sunken ship, didn't you?"

I stared at the man. I knew looting meant stealing. Was this guy a crook?

"What sunken ship?" the man demanded. "What are you talking about?"

"I think you know what I'm talking about, mate!" Officer Al said gruffly. "And as soon as we find your boat you're going to be charged with wreck-diving!"

"Wreck-diving?" I asked. "What's wreck-diving?"

Officer Lindy looked at me and smiled. "Divers sometimes hunt for ships under the sea," she explained. "But instead of alerting the government they loot the sunken ships and sell the artifacts."

"Who wants to buy old junk?" I asked. "It's probably all rusty from being in the water all that time."

"Some of the finds are very old and valuable,"

Officer Lindy said. "There are people who pay heaps of money for them, then sell them to foreign countries."

"Then what happens?" I asked.

"They often land up in museums," Officer Lindy said. "Or art galleries."

I pictured ancient objects I had seen in glass cases on school outings to Sydney museums.

"What's wrong with selling them to museums in different countries?" I asked. "Then everybody around the world can see them."

"The treasures are part of Australia's history. So wreck-divers aren't just robbing sunken Australian ships, they're robbing Australia of its heritage," she explained. "The museum curators who buy the stolen goods don't always know they're stolen."

"Wow," I said under my breath. Wreck-diving was serious stuff. But I still had questions, so I rushed after Officer Lindy as she walked back to the police boat.

"Wait, please!" I called. "How do wreck-divers know there's a sunken ship under the water?"

Officer Lindy was already in the boat when she shouted, "Sonar equipment! It's a wreck-diver's best friend!"

Sonar equipment? As in side scan sonars?

I stepped back as Officer Al hauled the man with the gashed leg into the boat.

"First we're going to fix that leg," Officer Al said. "Then you're going to lead us to your boat."

"Crikey," the man muttered.

I watched as the boat zoomed away.

"I'm sorry I shouted, 'Shark!'" I called after the boat.

As I turned I saw the crowd breaking up. The excitement for them was over. But not for me. That wreck-diver had me thinking about those pirates again! What if they were using side scan sonar to hunt for sunken ships? Maybe that's why Captain Dread flipped when I found it. They were doing something illegal!

In a way Elly was right, I thought. *Those pirates are on the hunt for sunken treasure!*

CHAPTER 11

I decided not to tell Dad about the Bondi Buccaneers and my wreck-diving theory. After what happened on the beach I didn't want to cause another panic!

But I was really itching to tell someone. So the morning I was back home on my own beach, I told Zara. "Guess what?" I asked as we walked on the sand. "I found out—"

"Me first! Me first!" Zara cut in.

I groaned as I balanced my surfboard under my arm. *There she goes again!*

"What?" I asked.

Zara took a suck of her lemon icypole

then said, "There was another beached dolphin yesterday. Not too far from where the other one was."

I bit my lip. While I was having fun in the sun, another poor dolphin was suffering. But maybe now I'd be able to help.

"Zara," I whispered. "I think I know the reason the whale and dolphins were beached."

"It's a no-brainer," Zara said. She pointed to the ocean with her icypole. "The weather changes are affecting the sea level. And all that rubbish in the water is making the fish sick."

"Yes," I said. "But whales and dolphins can also be confused by side scan sonar devices."

"Huh?" Zara asked. "What are you talking about?"

I stopped walking and leaned on my surfboard. "Sonar is sound waves under the sea," I explained. "Wreck-divers use scanners to search for sunken ships. Then they loot those ships and—"

"Wait a minute! Wait a minute," Zara interrupted. "What do underwater sound waves have to do with the environment?"

"It does when animals are endangered," I said. "And in a way, high frequency sound waves can be a sort of noise pollution."

Zara seemed to think about it as she sucked on her icypole. But then she shook her head and said, "I still think it's the drought and rubbish."

"Could be," I agreed. But that was my story and I was sticking to it!

I nodded toward the water and said, "I have a crave for a wave, Zara. See you later."

"Later," Zara said, her lips around her icypole.

My hair bounced on my shoulders as I raced with my board into the ocean. I popped up on my board. As the swell grew, so did my excitement.

"Grouse!" I cheered.

I was on top of the wave *and* the world. Until all of a sudden, from the corner of my eye I spotted the Plunderer's Pride!

If they do have stolen treasures, I thought as the wave carried me forward, *who are they selling it to?*

Woooooooooosh!

It was a monster wave I didn't see coming. I wiped out.

Luckily my board was attached to my foot with a leash. But by the time I surfaced, I was sputtering water out of my mouth and nose. Like all surfers, I had wiped out before. But this time I knew it was my fault. Instead of focusing on my moves I was thinking about the Bondi Buccaneers!

I pulled myself up on my board. As I paddled I glanced in the direction of the Plunderer's Pride. It was docked and empty.

Where did they go now? I wondered. As I carried my board out of the water, a high-pitched voice interrupted my thoughts. "Hellooooo!"

I turned and groaned. Standing on the beach and waving to me were the Aussie Glossie twins— Lucy and Darcy!

Lucy was wearing a Hawaiian print sarong over a plain black swimsuit. Darcy had on demin board shorts and a dotted bikini top.

"Hey," I said.

"We were watching you surf!" Lucy said.

"Yeah, I know. I wiped out," I said.

"No, you were awesome!" Darcy said. Lucy was nodding her head in agreement.

"Really?" I said, surprised. "Thanks."

"Was it hard to learn how to surf?" Lucy asked.

"At first," I said. "But after awhile I got the hang of it. You can take surfing lessons too!"

"Oh, we never go in the water," Darcy said, shaking her head. "I don't like seaweed much."

Lucy turned to her sister and frowned. "What are you talking about, Darcy?" she said. "You love the seaweed beauty wrap at the Aussie Glossie Spa!"

"Oops," Darcy giggled. "I forgot."

I didn't really want to chit-chat with the twins. But after such an awesome compliment I couldn't just walk away.

"So, have you been to the spa lately?" I asked to be polite. "I mean, since we talked over hot chocolate?"

"We wanted to go today," Lucy said with a frown. "But it's closed for the whole day."

"Our mum took us there for manicures," Darcy said. "But Madame Vera-Victoria turned everyone away."

"Not everyone, Darcy," Lucy told her. "Those grotty pirates were there!"

"Oops," Darcy giggled. "I forgot!"

I stared at Lucy and Darcy. Did they say pirates?

"What did they look like?" I asked.

"Mean and gross," Darcy said, rolling her eyes. "The big guy wore an eyepatch and had a smelly parrot on his shoulder."

Cecil, I thought. *Definitely the Bondi Buccaneers!*

"What are pirates going to do at a spa anyway?" Lucy scoffed. "Soak their feet in grog?"

Then she turned to her sister and said, "Come on, Darcy. Let's buy some of that glittery sunscreen we saw yesterday."

"Let's!" Darcy said excitedly.

As the twins walked away they waved to me and called, "Hooroo!"

"Hooroo to you too," I called back.

The twins' information was crash hot! The Bondi Buccaneers were at the Aussie Glossie Spa talking to Madame Vera-Victoria. And it must have been important for her to shut down the whole spa!

I leaned on my surfboard and stared out at the Plunderer's Pride.

I suddenly remembered the guy with the canvas sack running out of Madame's office. And the chat Madame had on the phone—about chains and convict ships!

Then I remembered something even more important. The rusty old compass Will gave me. The compass that was such a secret!

What *was* the secret? Did the compass come from a sunken Australian ship—a ship that was looted by wreck-divers? Could the pirates be selling the stolen loot to Madame Vera-Victoria?

There's definitely something fishy at the Aussie Glossie Spa, I decided. *And this time the sharks are for real!*

had to go to the Aussie Glossie Spa that day. No, not for a hot chocolate and marshmallow foot soak. To see what the Bondi Buccaneers and Madame Vera-Victoria were up to!

Since I wasn't allowed to go into the city alone, I talked Mum into taking me to work with her.

"Why do you want to go into the city today when you can be on the beach?" Mum asked. "In a few days you'll be back in school."

"I want to go to the Aussie Glossie Spa and say 'hi' to Will, the kid whose life I saved," I said. "You know…to make sure he doesn't have post-traumatic stress or something."

"Really?" Mum said with a smile. "I think I know the true reason you want to go to the Aussie Glossie Spa!"

My eyes popped wide open. Did Mum know I was on to something? Did Mum know I wanted to see what was going on behind Madame Vera-Victoria's closed doors?

"Y-you do?" I stammered.

"Yes!" Mum declared. She put her hands on my shoulders. "I think you loved your peanut butter facial and just don't want to admit it!"

"I…don't?" I asked.

"And you're hoping that Madame Vera-Victoria offers you another treatment!" Mum said.

I didn't want more peanut butter on my face and kiwi slices between my toes. But I didn't want to lie to Mum so I simply smiled and said, "Something like that!"

"Then let's go!" Mum declared.

I ran to my room and stepped into my uggies. Then I stashed my underwater camera into my bag. I wasn't planning on being underwater, but the camera took land shots too.

Feeling like a spy on a mission, I rode the bus with Mum to her travel agency. A couple from Holland was there to plan a trip. They wanted to take a train ride from one side of Australia all the way to the other!

"That would take sixty-five hours," Mum said.

"So long?" the Dutch woman gasped.

"We do not have that much time," the man said.

"Australia is a huge continent," Mum explained. "But I can arrange a lovely flight to Alice Springs in the Outback."

I watched Mum at work. She was really getting the hang of her new job. But I had a job to do too. A very important job!

"Pardon, Mum?" I asked as she poured the couple two cups of coffee. "May I visit Will now?"

"Sure, Pip," Mum said. "And good luck with Madame Vera-Victoria!"

I smiled at the Dutch couple then left the travel agency. My boots made clop-clop-clopping sounds as I ran down the block. When I reached the Aussie Glossie Spa, I saw Cecil perched on the front gate. Now I knew the pirates were inside the spa!

"What's up, Cecil?" I asked.

"Arrrrk!" Cecil screeched. "Stash the loot, stash the loot, raaaak!"

Loot, huh? I grinned at Cecil as I opened the front gate. The pieces were starting to fall into place.

As I walked up the stone path, I could see Will sitting on the front steps. He was staring down at a handheld video game and mumbling as he pressed the keys. "In your face, space-case!"

"G'day, Will," I said.

Will looked up from his game and smiled. "I just blasted thirty alien invaders from Planet Zagon!" he said. "Am I brilliant or what?"

"Way brilliant!" I said. "Where's your gran?"

"Inside the spa," Will answered. "She wanted me to wait out here until after her customers left."

I sat down next to Will and asked, "Are the customers dressed like pirates?"

"Yeah!" Will replied. "How did you know?"

I nodded at Cecil scratching his feathery belly with his beak. "A little birdy told me," I said.

"You mean him?" Will said, glancing at Cecil. "You're lucky that's all he did—because he pecked my nose!"

"Raaaaak!" Cecil screeched.

While Will stuck his tongue out at Cecil I decided to get down to business. "Will, can you tell me where you got that compass you gave me?" I asked.

"I told you!" Will said, shaking his head. "It's a secret!"

Will was going to be a tough nut to crack. But I wasn't going to cop out. "Come on, Will," I said. "You said you owe me, remember?"

"Gee whiz!" Will exclaimed. "Doesn't the compass count?"

"That was a prezzie," I said with a smile. "You still owe me a favor."

Will heaved a big sigh. Then he stood up.

"Okay," Will said in a hushed voice. "But we can't let my grandmother see us. What I'm about to show you is top secret."

"Top secret, top secret!" Cecil squawked. "Arrrrk!"

"Will you shut up?" Will hissed.

I stood up too. Will slipped his game into the pocket of his jumper (sweater). Then he opened the door and waved me inside.

As we stepped inside the pale blue entrance hall there was no woman in a white coat to greet us. No fairies either. Just a big empty building with Madame Vera-Victoria's voice echoing through it!

"Why would I shell out good money for a rusty key?" Madame's voice snapped.

"It's the key to a shackle, Vera!" another voice said. "You said you wanted convict stuff so there you have it!"

My arms and legs stiffened. I knew Captain Dread's snarky voice anywhere!

"Come on," Will whispered. "Before my grandmother comes out of her office!"

We raced down a hallway past doors marked, Wax n' Relax, Meditation Maison and Pedi Palace. The Pampered Princess Parlour didn't need a sign —it reeked of sugar and peanuts!

Will stopped next to Madame's office. He tiptoed quickly past her door, than waved to me to do the same. It wasn't easy tiptoeing in chunky boots but

I did it like a champ. On my way past Madame's office I couldn't help but sneak a little peak. There they were—the pirates sitting in front of Madame's desk with their backs to the door.

Behind the desk stood Madame, counting the large wad of money in her hands... "Three hundred...four hundred..." Will tugged me away from the door. "I thought you want to see where I got the compass!" he hissed.

"I do!" I whispered back.

When we reached the end of the hall, Will opened another door. Through it was a dark staircase leading downstairs.

"Where does it go?" I asked.

"To the basement," Will answered. "You go first."

It felt creepy walking down in the dark. But halfway down the stairs, Will flipped on a light switch. When I reached the basement it smelled musty and dusty. Kind of like the inside of a vintage clothing store!

Looking around I didn't see old clothes or shoes. Instead there were rows of metal shelves filled with bottles, colored jars, pewter plates and goblets.

"Most of it's old junk," Will said.

I didn't say a word as I walked to one of the shelves. Picking up a pewter pitcher I read the words stamped on the bottom: H.M. King George III.

"King George III of England?" I asked myself.

I flashed back to my history studies at school. King George III reigned in the eighteenth century. That was thc 1700's!

"This stuff isn't old junk, Will," I said. "These are ancient treasures!"

CHAPTER 13

Will watched as I searched the shelves. I could tell he didn't get why I was so interested. But I was finding more than just bottles and goblets. I found glass beads, clay pipes, a velvet box filled with copper coins and two pairs of heavy iron shackles.

"I think those were used to keep prisoners from walking," Will said.

"I know," I said.

I thought about my ancestor Benjamin Whelan. He probably didn't wear shackles if he was able to swim to shore. But it still must have been horrible to be taken far, far away from your homeland.

"This is where I got your compass," Will said, pointing around the room. "It was the only thing that still worked."

While I checked out a clay pipe, Will picked up an old copper coin.

"I wonder how many packs of chewie (gum) I could get with this," Will said.

"Will?" I asked. "Where did your gran get all this stuff?"

"I don't know," Will said, flipping the coin in his hand. "When I told my grandmother I found this room she made me promise to keep it a secret."

Will smirked a bit and added, "As you can see I'm not very good at keeping secrets!"

I reached to place the pipe back on the shelf and knocked down a pewter plate. Will cringed as it clattered across the floor.

"If my grandmother finds us down here she'll be totally narky (upset)!" Will whispered. "Let's get out of here now!"

"Okay, you go ahead," I said. "I just want to put back the plate."

I let Will walk halfway up the stairs. Then I pulled my camera out of my bag and snapped about three pictures of the treasures.

"Proof!" I whispered.

I was just about to run up the stairs when I remembered the plate. I picked it up and placed it carefully on one of the shelves.

"Pip!" Will called out. "Are you coming or what?"

"Coming!" I bounded toward him.

Will looked relieved as he shut the door to the basement. I didn't want to pass Madame Vera-Victoria's office again. What if she saw me this time? What if the pirates saw me?

"Is there a side door, Will?" I asked.

"Sure," Will said. "This way."

Once outside I saw Cecil perched on a bush. The parrot's beady little eye blinked as he stared sideways at me.

"Thanks for showing me where you got my compass, Will," I said.

"No problem," Will said. "But why did you want to know?"

I didn't want Will to know I was spying on his grandmother. So I just smiled and said, "Because I never saw anything like it before!"

Will said goodbye and went inside. Cecil was still blinking at me as I began walking along the side of the house. "What are you looking at, cracker breath?" I muttered.

"Cracker breath! Cracker breath! Arrrk!" Cecil screeched.

I was just racing around the house when I saw the front door swing open. Ducking behind the house I peeked out. The pirates and Madame Vera-Victoria were stepping out of the spa.

Bruce licked his finger as he counted a large wad of money. "Three hundred...four hundred—"

"Put that away before someone sees it!" Dread

said, jabbing Bruce with his elbow.

"Yes, be careful," Madame said. "Is anyone on to you?"

"Just some kid," Dread answered. "She's been snooping around the boat and asking questions."

Jingoes, I thought. *They're talking about me!*

"Some kid, eh?" Madame said. "Well, just make sure she doesn't know too much."

"She's a kid, Vera," Bruce said. "What are we supposed to do?"

"Get rid of her!" Madame barked. "Take her out to sea and throw her to the sharks!"

"Heh, heh," Connie snickered. "Good one, Vera!"

"I wasn't joking!" Madame snapped. "Oh, and Connie dear, you must come back to the spa for a full lip and chin wax…unless you're *trying* to look like Blackbeard the Pirate."

"What?" Connie squeaked.

"Have a nice day!" Madame said cheerily. "And remember—more convict loot!"

I could hear her slam the door shut. I was hoping the pirates would leave next—until I saw Cecil still blinking at me.

"Cecil, ye blabberin' scurvy squawker!" Dread shouted out. "Get your feathered tail over here!"

My heart pounded inside my chest. What if

Captain Dread came back here to look for Cecil? And found me instead?

Cecil gave a little squawk. Then he flapped his feathery wings, flew off the bush and shot around the house.

"Thank you!" I said under my breath.

I listened as the front gate creaked open. Captain Dread, Bruce and Connie were leaving at last. And at last I knew the truth. The Bondi Buccaneers were looting sunken ships for valuable relics! I was certain they were using side scan sonars to do it. And they were hurting the whales and dolphins.

And the person buying those relics was the owner of the Aussie Glossie Spa – Madame Vera-Victoria!

I slipped around the house and shot out the front gate. The pirates were gone, but I wasn't safe yet. They were definitely on to me, but I couldn't stop now. No way! I had to save the whales, the dolphins —and Australian history!

It was hard not telling Mum about my secret mission. But if I told Mum, she'd tell Dad and Dad would tell me not to cause a panic. And if I told Elly she'd tell the whole world!

It won't be easy, I decided. *But I have to keep my mouth shut.*

While Mum worked, I sat in the far corner of her office checking out the pictures I took of the ancient artifacts.

"Pip?" Mum called from her desk. "If those are the underwater pictures you took at the Great Barrier Reef, I want to see them."

Gulp.

I looked out from behind the computer monitor and said, "Um…this is just boring stuff you don't want to see, Mum."

"If you say so," Mum sighed.

She went back to stuffing a file folder, and I went back to my pictures. The ancient artifacts from the sunken ship came out crystal clear!

I have proof of the stolen loot, I thought. *Now all I need is proof of the side scan sonar.*

But in order to do that I would have to go back on the Plunderer's Pride.

The thought of coming face-to-face with Captain Dread was enough to make my teeth curl. What if he really did make me walk the plank? I'm a good swimmer—but not with my legs and arms tied together!

My heart began to race as I pictured the scene inside my head.

I can't do it! I thought in a panic. *Somebody else*

will just have to save Australian history, that's all.

But when I thought about the poor beached mammals, I caved. Somebody had to do something to save those dolphins and whales.

And that somebody was me!

CHAPTER 14

The next day was Sunday and that meant Nippers. Zac taught us some stuff about first aid, then we had a paddling race on our surfboards.

While my board raced, my mind did too—with thoughts about the Bondi Buccaneers. I was determined to find a way to get on that boat. As soon as Nippers was over, I would snap some shots of the side scan sonar with the underwater camera I wore around my neck and—

"Hey!" a voice interrupted my thoughts.

I turned my head and saw a woman waving her hand and bobbing up and down in the water.

"Hey, hey!" she shouted again.

I stopped paddling. The woman looked like she needed help!

"I'm coming! I'm coming!" I shouted.

I broke away from my group and began paddling my surfboard toward the drowning woman.

"Pip!" Zac shouted from the beach. "Get back in the race. Right now!"

For a surf lifesaver, Zac was pretty clueless—

this woman was in distress!

By the time I reached the woman she was staring bug-eyed at me. Probably in shock!

"Don't worry, ma'am!" I said, leaning over my board and grabbing her arm. "I've got you now." I tried pulling the woman on my surfboard but she wouldn't budge.

"I'm not drowning!" the woman insisted.

"But…you were waving and jumping up and down like a 'roo!" I said.

"I was waving to my husband on the beach," the woman said, pointing. "He's over there!"

I looked to see a man smiling from the sand. Oops.

I let go of the woman's arm. I felt really stupid. I couldn't even warn the woman about her sunburn, because she was coated with sunscreen and zinc!

"G'day," I said, forcing a smile.

The race was over so I paddled my board to shore.

"My hero!" one of my Nipper mates teased as I carried my surfboard out of the water.

But Zac wasn't joking when he said, "Pip, I know you were a hero the other day, and I know Nippers are all about beach safety, but you can't leave the group like that."

"Sorry," I sighed. "I guess I just have a lot on my mind today."

"Do you want to be excused for the rest of the morning?" Zac asked gently.

My eyes lit up. No Nippers meant more time to search the Plunderer's Pride!

"That would be great, Zac," I said. I realized I sounded a bit too excited so I quickly added, "I mean, that would be the best thing to do I suppose."

"Okay," Zac said. "But go straight to your dad's shack."

"My dad's shack—yeah," I agreed.

Zac and the Nippers fell in line for a run on the beach. Some of the kids smiled back at me as they ran. I smiled too as I pulled off my striped cap.

Any other day I would have loved hanging with Zac and my Nipper mates. But today I had a whole different sort of rescuing to do.

I ran straight to Dad's Surf Shack to drop off my board and explain that I had the morning off. Dad seemed concerned until I told him I was feeling fine—just wanted some time to myself.

"You know…to surf," I said.

"Okay," Dad said. He then nodded to the camera hanging around my neck. "What's that for?"

"Oh," I said, trying to think fast. "Just in case I see something interesting." Like the side scan sonar or stolen treasures!

I began to walk away from the shack when Dad called, "Wait!"

I froze in my tracks. Did Dad suspect I was about to do something dangerous? "Yeah, Dad?" I asked.

"Don't forget your surfboard," Dad said.

"My surfboard!" I said, running to my board and picking it up. "Du-uh!"

But what was I going to do with my board on the Plunderer's Pride?

As I walked across the beach with my board under my arm, I saw Elly and her Nippers splashing in the water. Elly thought I was such a hero. If she only knew I was about to do the most heroic thing in my life.

Heroic…or stupid! I thought. Then I kept walking toward the marina and the Plunderer's Pride.

I didn't see the pirates as I walked up the dock to the boat. I did see a handwritten sign stuck on the boat that read, BACK IN AN HOUR, MATIES!

An hour? I wondered. *When did they put up the sign?*

I decided to take a chance and search the boat. I didn't want to leave my board on the dock so I tossed it into the boat. Then I jumped in after it.

My heart pounded inside my chest as I stood on the deck of the Plunderer's Pride—but I couldn't waste time. I leaned my board against one of the benches and quickly got to work.

I last saw the side scan sonar and the black box behind the big plastic trunk. The trunk was still there but when I ran behind it they were both gone!

Maybe they're inside the trunk! I thought.

Opening the lid, I peered inside. It was still filled

with diving gear and— "The rocket-shaped gizmo!" I cheered under my breath. "Ye-es!"

I aimed my camera at the gizmo but the sonar device was too far back for me to get a good shot. Glancing around I spotted a metal bucket nearby. I dragged it to the trunk, flipped it over and climbed up on it. From there I was able to zero in on the sonar device and black box.

Smiling I took the shot. I got the gizmo and the words Seahalk Sonar Device stamped on the side. You couldn't get better proof than that! Now all I had to do was get off the boat and bring all my pictures to the police!

"Unreal!" I said excitedly.

But just as I was about to jump off the bucket I heard voices… "If you ask me, Vera low-balled us!"

"Yeah, she should have coughed up more for those pocket watches!"

My blood froze. It was the pirates!

I had no time to look for a hiding place. So I jumped inside the trunk and reached up to close the lid.

"Rats!" I hissed. The lid was too high for me to reach. I tossed aside the clunky side scan sonar and buried myself under wetsuits and flippers!

Phew! The air inside the trunk smelled like

rubber, sea water and sweat. But as the pirates' voices got louder and louder, I crouched down lower and lower.

"You heard what Vera said," Captain Dread said. "She wants more convict loot so she can sell them to museums in Europe and America."

"Vera, Vera," Bruce sighed. "Why does she have to have a piece of the action anyway?"

"Because we're working for her!" Captain Dread said. "Who do you think set us up with this lame whale-watching racket in the first place?"

Aha! I thought. *The Bondi Buccaneers was just a front for what the pirates really did—wreck-diving!*

I knew I had to get off the boat—but how?

Suddenly I heard Captain Dread demand in a loud, growling voice, "Oi—where did this come from?"

"Any of you blokes take up surfing?" Bruce chuckled.

Surfing…my surfboard! I had totally forgotten about my surfboard on the deck for everybody to see!

"Ya think someone's on the boat?" Connie asked.

I held my breath as I heard the pirates trodding across the deck.

Maybe they won't find me, I thought hopefully. *Maybe they'll just throw my board out of the boat, and I'll sneak off the boat after they leave—*

"Raaak!"

I glanced up. Perched on the edge of the trunk with ruffled feathers was Cecil the parrot!

"Get lost!" I hissed.

"Get lost! Get lost!" Cecil screeched. "Arrrk!"

Gulping hard, I sank into the diving gear. I knew I was busted—especially when all three of the Bondi Buccaneers surrounded the trunk!

"Um…hi, guys!" I squeaked as I pretended to dig through the gear. "Still looking for that Nipper badge!"

Captain Dread flashed a wicked smile.

"Well, what do you know, boys!" he snarled. "We got ourselves a little stowaway!"

onnie and Bruce pulled me out of the trunk. Captain Dread wasn't wearing his eyepatch so he glared at me with both steely-blue eyes.

"What were you doing in there?" Dread demanded. He pointed to the camera around my neck. "And don't tell me you were looking for your Nipper badge with that camera!"

I had to think fast. Real fast.

"Actually, I was looking for my surfboard this time." I faked surprise as I pointed to it. "Oh, and there it is!"

I began walking toward my board when Dread stepped in front of me. "I may look batty in this pirate get-up—but I'm no fool!" he snapped. "You've been snooping and you'd better tell me why!"

I was scared. So scared even my freckles must have paled. But I couldn't let the pirates see me sweat. So I threw back my shoulders, took a deep breath and said, "Not until you tell me why you're using a side scan sonar device on your boat. The one you stashed in the trunk over there!" The pirates stared at the trunk, then at each other. "So?" I asked again. "What are you using sonar equipment for?"

"What's the big deal?" Connie asked me. She pulled the sonar device out of the trunk and held it up. "We're a whale watching boat so we look for whales under the water!"

"You're not looking for whales," I said. "You're hurting the whales and dolphins with that stupid gizmo of yours!"

The pirates began to laugh.

"Well!" Dread boomed. "Not only do we have a stowaway, we've got ourselves a Greenie!"

"Are you a Greenie, girlie?" Connie chuckled.

I narrowed my eyes at Connie. "Are you a wreck-diver…girlie?" I sneered.

Silence.

With daggers shooting from her eyes, Connie dropped the side scan sonar on the bench.

"What do you know about the wreck?" Dread demanded.

"Everything I need to know," I said.

Was I being brave—or crazy? Something told me I was about to find out.

"Should I take her camera?" Bruce asked.

My hand clapped my camera against my chest. But Captain Dread shook his head.

"You heard what Vera said," Dread muttered to his mates. "Take her out."

"Take me out?" I demanded. "What do you mean?"

Connie pushed my shoulder until I sat hard on the bench. As I watched Bruce and Dread untie the boat my mouth turned as dry as fairy floss (cotton candy). The pillaging pirates were taking me out to sea to do what Vera told them to do: Throw me to the sharks!

Connie's nails dug into my shoulder as I turned around. I could see Bondi Beach shrinking smaller and smaller as the Plunderer's Pride zoomed further and further into the waters. My eyes darted back and forth as I looked for Dad's Surf Shack.

There it is!

Dad looked as small as a speck, but I could see him waxing a surfboard. My mouth opened to yell, "Daaaaad!" But nothing came out. I may have acted brave in front of the pirates, but deep inside I was shaking in my uggies. Would I ever see my family again? Go to school again?

My breath came out faster and faster as I took in the smell of salty sea water. It had always given me a warm and fuzzy feeling inside. Now it just made me want to chuck!

I'm not even wearing a life jacket, I thought.

But what difference would a life jacket make when you were about to lose your life?

I jumped as Cecil landed on the bench next to me. First he rolled his head around and around, then squawked, "Raaaak!"

"What do *you* want?" I muttered.

Cecil blinked at me and squawked softly. Was that an apology for ratting me out?

I couldn't look at the beach anymore, so I turned my head slowly. That's when I saw it—a gigantic wave swelling in the distance!

Connie must have seen it too, because her hand dropped from my shoulder. Bruce was standing up in the cabin, frantically operating the controls. As for Captain Dread, he picked up his eye patch and stared frozen at the monster wave.

"Cheese and scallawaggin' crackers!" Dread exclaimed.

"Raaaaak!" Cecil's feathers began to ruffle as if he smelled danger too.

The pirates began scrambling on deck as the wave towered over the boat. I jumped to my feet. Then with a whoosh—the monster wave crashed into the Plunderer's Pride!

"Ahhhhhhh!"
Dread yelled as the
wave hit.

The boat lurched
and all three pirates
stumbled and rolled
across the deck.

I stumbled too but
I didn't fall. Instead
my feet jumped
apart, my knees
bent and I began
steadying myself
against the rocking
deck. "Bonza!" I
yelled. I may have
been on a boat, but
my surfie skills were
kicking in—big time!

The pirates tried to stand up, only to fall down
again. But as soon as the wave flattened I could see
the three scrambling to their feet. Captain Dread's
eyes burned with anger when he saw me standing.

Uh-oh, I thought.

My stomach was doing serious flips and it
wasn't because I was seasick. I was sick with the

fear of being shark chum!

But as scared as I was, I knew I had to act fast. I grabbed the heavy side scan sonar off the bench. Then I hurled it with all my might. The silver gizmo rocketed through the air before dropping straight in the pirate's path!

"Whoa!" Dread cried as he tripped over the device. The captain's feet flew up in the air, then he landed with a thud on his pirate's booty!

Dread was down for the count. And I had to get off the boat any way I could!

But as my eyes darted around I knew there was only one way off the Plunderer's Pride— *overboard*!

In a flash I grabbed my surfboard. With the Bondi Buccaneers on my heels I ran to the side and scrambled up on the bench. I tucked my board under my arm and jumped into the ocean with a giant SPLASH!

I could hear the pirates shouting as I pulled myself up on my surfboard. Trying to block out their voices, I steadied myself and waited for the next wave.

"Come on, come on, come on!" I said under my breath. *Where was a monster wave when you needed one to save your life?*

As if the ocean could hear me, a wave started to swell, rising up under my board. My back jerked as the wave swept me forward. Bending my knees and steadying my arms, I matched the speed of the swell sweeping me away from the Plunderer's Pride!

"She's getting away!" Dread shouted.

I was going so fast I couldn't yell back at the pirates, but if I could I probably would have said, "Ha! You didn't know I was a Greenie and a Surfie, ya bilge-sucking wreck-diving bandits!"

From the face of the wave, I could see Bondi Beach growing nearer and nearer in the distance. Home sweet home!

"Woo-hooooo!" I cheered.

But just as I started lightening up, I lost my footing and my board. My stomach rose into my chest as my board and I tumbled off the face of the wave. The roaring rush of the ocean turned into dead silence as I sank deep beneath the water. I didn't have enough time to hold my breath so I frantically scissored my legs until I reached the surface.

Gasp! I sucked in every drop of air I could get. Then I looked around for my surfboard. All I could see was a stretch of blue ocean between me and Bondi Beach.

I tried waving for a surf lifesaver but it was too far for anyone to see me. What was I going to do—other than try to swim it myself?

I'm a good swimmer, I thought. *I can do it.*

Kicking my legs and pumping my arms I swam toward the beach. But the more I swam, the more tired I got. Until my arms and legs felt as heavy as cement.

"Just…a…bit…further," I gasped to myself. "I…can…do…it."

It was no use. My body became an anchor as I began to go under. But for some strange reason I didn't panic. Instead I saw my family inside my head—my dad waxing his surfboards, Elly running after me on the beach, and my Mum saying, "You can't save the whole world, Pip!"

Save the world? Ha.

I couldn't even save myself!

CHAPTER 16

As I sank deeper and deeper, someone else popped inside my head. Someone I never saw before but knew very well. It was my great-great-great-too-great-to-count grandfather Benjamin Whelan.

I couldn't see his face or hear his voice. I could only feel his strength—the same strength he must have had when he swam from his ship hundreds of years ago! If he had given up, I wouldn't even be here.

If he could do it, I can do it!

Then with Benjamin Whelan's gritty blood pumping through my veins, I swam and swam until I finally reached the surface.

First I took a big gulp of salty sea air. Then I began swimming toward the beach—full speed ahead!

Benjamin Whelan's Irish accent cheered me on inside my head. After what seemed like forever, I finally reached the shallow waters of Bondi Beach!

I tried to stand up but my legs were too wobbly. Luckily I didn't have to because there to pull me in was Zac—and my fellow Nippers!

"Hang on, Pip," Zac said as he picked me up and carried me to shore.

I looked up as I lay on the sand. The sun was in my eyes so I couldn't see who was standing around me, but judging from the noise around me, I had a pretty big audience!

"I guess that's the last time you'll surf that far out, eh?" Zac asked me.

"I *didn't* surf all the way out!" I said. "I was kidnapped by pirates who wanted to throw me to the sharks!"

"Pirates?" a man's voice whispered.

"I think she's a bit delirious," a woman whispered. "Poor thing."

But then I heard a familiar voice. It was Dad saying, "Pip? What are you talking about?"

I shaded the sun from my eyes with my hands. Dad and Elly were standing over me. I knew they must have thought I had kangaroos loose in the paddock. But I couldn't stop telling what I knew was the truth…

"The Bondi Buccaneers are wreck-divers, Dad," I said, trying to sit up. "They're using a side scan sonar on their boat that's hurting the whales and dolphins!"

"How do you know?" Dad asked.

Uh-oh. How was I going to prove that I saw the side scan sonar? And Madame Vera-Victoria's secret room of stolen treasures?

That's when I remembered the camera—still hanging around my neck. The camera had flipped around and was hanging down my back so I had almost forgotten it was there.

"Not only do I know, Dad," I said as I patted the trusty camera. "I have proof!"

"Wowee! Way to go, Pip!" Elly cheered, jumping up and down. "You're a hero—and a super spy!"

"And a ripper swimmer!" Zac said with a wink.

I wanted to tell them about hearing Benjamin Whelan cheering me on—but I decided not to. Pirates were crazy enough, but 300 year-old ghosts—that would really sound crazy!

So after drinking a bottle of water and eating two energy bars, Dad brought me straight to the police station. There I told them everything I knew about the Bondi Buccaneers and Madame Vera-Victoria.

After hearing my story and looking at my pictures, the police had everything they needed to bring the pirates in for kidnapping, wreck-diving and animal cruelty. Madame Vera-Victoria was arrested for her part too.

"It's my fault," Will said while he waited for his parents at the police station. "If I hadn't shown you the secret room none of this would have happened. How could I be so stupid?"

"You're not stupid. You're a hero," I told Will. "Think of all the whales and dolphins you saved. And the treasures that will be kept in Australia where they belong!"

Will shrugged as if he didn't care. But I had a feeling he would someday.

And in case you're wondering about Cecil the

parrot, he was taken in too. Not by the police—by Zara as a pet! She couldn't wait for her foster-koala so a parrot was the perfect answer. Now instead of squawking like a bilge-sucking pirate, good ol' Cecil will be squawking like a true Greenie in no time!

And guess what? There really was a sunken ship that the pirates were looting. Divers invited Dad and me to see the ship I saved.

The name of the ship was the HMS Primrose. Sound familiar? It's the same ship that brought my great-great-great-too-great-to-count grandfather Benjamin Whelan to Australia 300 years ago!

So not only did I, Pipper the Ripper Nipper, save the whales and the dolphins, I saved an important part of Australian history.

...*And my own!*

Learn more about me and the
Land Down Under by reading from my journal!

Dad and Mum gave me this great new underwater camera. It was a thoughtful little prezzy and a real ripper. I can take pics of my friends and anything I want. I have to share with my little ankle biter of a sister, Elly. She can be a real stickybeak sometimes, but she's my sissy... follows me everywhere!

THERE ARE LOTS OF ROOS...

My family is from Australia! I live at Bondi Beach, right close to Sydney. Greatest surfing in the whole-wide-world. Dad has the greatest surf shop in the world. Mum works as a travel agent in the city. Me, I just love the beach—surfing with my mates.

...AND DIDGERIDOOS TOO!

Can I tell you how much I love surfing? When I'm not in school, or helping Dad out around his surf shack, I'm on the beaches. I can "hang-5," but not 10, not yet, anyway! That means hangin' five toes off the front end of your board. I'm getting better 'cause I practice every day.

SURF AND SUN SUNBLOCK SPF 40

MY FRIEND ZARA

SUNSCREEN!

ZARA

Didn't mean to give you an ear bashin' 'bout the greatest sport down under. For surfing all you need is your board, a comfy cozzie (swim suit), and off you go. Sometimes a wet suit comes in handy because the ocean water can get very cold.

I joined the Bondi Beach Nippers when I was only 7 years old. They were Australia's first official surf lifesaving club, and first in the world. They started at Bondi in 1906. We learn about safe swimming and lifesaving techniques. We play lots of games, too!

Product	Product Code	Sizes	Description	Price
Skull Caps	SBSKULL	OSFM - Child	One size fits most skull cap	$8.80
Boy's surf briefs	BHPLB	6 to 14	Boy's swimmers. Fully lined	$15.00
Girl's racing swimmers	SWPLG1	6 to 14	Girl's one piece swimmers. Fully lined	$28.95
Rash Guards	RGPLY	4 to 8	Unisex rash guard. Flatlock stitching with rubber waist.	$19.60
Rash Guards	RGPLY	10 to 14	Unisex rash guard. Flatlock stitching with rubber waist.	$20.50
Girl's racing singlet	SGPLG	4 to 8	Girl's plain singlet Flatlock stitching. with rubber waist.	$22.75
Girl's racing singlet	SGPLG	10 to 14	Girl's plain singlet Flatlock stitching, with rubber waist.	$24.75
Boy's racing singlet	SGTBB	4 to 8	Boy's plain singlet Flatlock stitching, with rubber waist, arms & neck.	$22.
Boy's racing singlet	SGTBB	10 to 14	Boy's plain singlet Flatlock stitching, with rubber waist, arms & neck.	$

YOU CAN SPOT US, EASY-PEASY, WITH OUR CAPS!

Whenever I'm walking down the sandy and see some bloke throw down his trash, I think to myself, what a bludger! There are recycling bins right on the beach. Wish there were more. I tell people we are choking the earth with so many water bottles, and aren't cloth nappies just as good as the throw away kind?

THEY LOOK LIKE SKULLS~

AUSTRALIA COMPARED WITH THE UNITED STATES OF AMERICA

I don't think people realize how big Australia is, and the impact we could have if we all just helped out a little more. I know I can't change the world by myself, but I can make a difference. So can you!

RECYCLE

THAT'S WHAT THEY CALL ME!

AUSTRALIA
GREENIE

My family has been in Australia for many generations. Great, great, great, too-great to-count Grandfather Whelan came to the "Lucky Island" from Ireland for stealing a cow. He was just trying to feed his family. His ship wrecked just before they arrived. Swimmers run in my family!

A CONVICT FISH!

Yes, Australia was settlled by convicts from England. They came on ships like this. It was a difficult voyage and many died along the way. It took brave men to make the trip. It was uncharted territory, almost like going to the moon. They would say, "at least from England, you could see the moon!"

Mum used her travel agent mojo to score a family scuba diving trip to the Great Barrier Reef. Dad even closed up the surf shop for a holiday. The reef is a magical underwater world. We saw plants and animals that exist nowhere else in the world. Scuba diving is almost as fun as surfing! Gave my camera a workout.

DIVER DOWN

The reef has suffered from all the curious, but well-meaning tourists. Never, never, never should you break off a piece of coral as a souvenir. What if everyone did that? In no time at all there'd be nothing left to enjoy. With global temps on the rise the coral is bleaching. YIKES!

The saddest sight I have ever seen is a beached whale. It breaks my heart! Usually it happens when they are sick, but more and more because of pollution and misuse of sonar equipment, these beautiful animals become confused and wind up ashore. Sometimes the Nippers get to help with the rescue.

When the Nippers helped the marine biologist load the beached whale onto a truck to transport her to a place where she could get better, I almost forgot to snap a picture. By the time I found my camera, all that was left of the scene were the little Nipper prints in the sand.
Still, it made me happy to help.

After I rescued a boy that got knocked off his board, his grateful gran gave me a day pass to come visit her salon called THE AUSSIE GLOSSIE SPA. It's in Sydney, but close to Mum's office, and very close to the opera house. Mum said I could go and gave me some money for the day, so off I went.

Well that was quite an an adventure. The goop they put on my face smelled like peanuts. Ick! Give me my sunnies (sunglasses) & some sand between my toes and I'm happy as a clam. At least I got my nails painted an earth-friendly shade of green. And I still caught some waves before dinner!